AMERICAN HISTORY 101

Conspiracy Nation

Mike Palecek

CWG Press

Published by
CWG Press
1517 NE 5th Ter #1
Fort Lauderdale, FL 33304
www.cwgpress.com

ISBN 13: 978-0-9788186-8-5

Printed in the U.S.A.

"I knew that a historian (or a journalist, or anyone telling a story) was forced to choose, out of an infinite number of facts, what to present, what to omit. And that decision inevitably would reflect, whether consciously or not, the interests of the historian."
— Howard Zinn, *A People's History of the United States: 1492 to Present*

"The crimes of the United States have been systematic, constant, vicious, remorseless, but very few people have actually talked about them. You have to hand it to America. It has exercised a quite clinical manipulation of power worldwide while masquerading as a force for universal good.

"It's a brilliant, even witty, highly successful act of hypnosis. I put to you that the United States is without doubt the greatest show on the road."
— Harold Pinter, Nobel Prize For Literature speech, "Art, Truth and Politics," 2005

CHAPTER ONE

"Never look back unless you are planning to go that way."
— Henry David Thoreau

The sharp-eyed, white-headed eagle circled, silently, stealthily, around and around, wings outstretched, small circle to big circle, securing the perimeter, concentric coils of security.

Metallic blue eyes clanked and whirred and locked for a moment on the painted image of the griffin at the fifty-yard line of the high school football field, the hybrid mascot for the consolidated high schools of the adjoining little bergs along the winding Greenberg River: New Cumbria, New Angus, New Broom, New Fife, New Greenham.

Locals just called it New Town.

The eagle saw everything, so it must know everything, right?

It zoomed in, out, as a camera recording, writing into its brain all that it saw.

In a downtown neighborhood a man ran from a house, leaping the steps while his pistol blazed at those on the sidewalk, in the bushes.

The reports barked like fireworks, leaving the tall man stretched on his side, still in running pose, red mixing with the green, Christmas colors.

The driver of the ambulance in the street turned on his lights, hit the siren, flipped it off. He climbed down, waited with one foot on the asphalt for the cameramen to get their last shots.

"Okay."

He nodded to his helper and they wheeled the gurney across the bumpy lawn, around the lights, director, producer, extras. They stretched on blue gloves, expertly enveloped the body with the black bag, took safety precautions, bent knees, straight back to lift at least until their knees hurt as they had both been to a recent workshop, tossed the body onto the gurney and this time followed the goddamned walk.

"Print Is Dead?" said the short, dumpy man, balding, twanging his suspenders against his chest as he slapped the magazine onto the desk.

"Print Is Dead" said the headline on the cover of the four-color glossy industry magazine.

Nikostatos Greenberg paced in his office, trailing cigar smoke, turning and running into the smoke, away from it, back again.

The tarnished plate on the softball trophy on the desk with pitcher in underhand motion said "Nick Green, ol' Fireball."

His memories hanged on the wood panel, black and white family photos, blending into '70s color and stopping ten years ago, halfway down the west wall.

Lined up by the door were fishing poles, tackle boxes, fishing hats, waders, and a neat stack of crisp fishing magazines. A giant moose loomed right over his desk with the nose almost in the doorway, that had twenty nicknames, and where exactly it had come from was the object of some debate.

Green stopped to look out the windows, hands on hips.

He adjusted his Yankees cap, puffed the cigar, his stomach sandwich stains in the face of the man seated at Nick's desk and his back to those gathered for the production meeting.

Nick Green looked, but did not see.

He picked at his fingernails. Nobody ever said anything. They must not notice.

In his search for something he adjusted his cap, picked more at his fingernails, scrunched his nose like a worried rabbit and placed his hand for a moment on his thumping heart.

He searched for answers, but not in the smoke rising from the factory stacks of the publishing house that lay in New Fife right on the river.

It had been a real publishing house back then, a house overlooking the river, in the middle of a field, with many floors and offices and cozy dens for writing and thinking and drawing and the craft of making something special to last for decades.

"Who said?" said one of those behind Nick.

"The Easter Bunny!" Nick spun with a laugh, big arms and smile, spot on that comment just as it was delivered as he had hoped.

Around him sat the department heads on metal folding chairs they had brought themselves: Michelle Jones, Editing; Lori Groome, Art; Walt Anderson, Printing; Kolya Zuyev, Wood Products; Amos Chadwick, Research & Writing; Buddy Fowler, Maintenance & Landscaping; Cade Ewart, Crowd Control/Security; Kathryn (Bambi) Cartwright, HR/PR.

In Nick Green's rickety rolling wooden chair behind the desk sat Austin Bellincioni, lead accountant for Beantree Barkham Bagnor ... Kruszynianys, hunched over a yellow legal pad, occasionally punching with two fingers at an adding machine he had brought from his office specifically for this meeting.

Each of the department heads held in their laps the latest issue of *Book Publishing Right Now*.

"Rrrring!" sprang the black phone in the outer office.

Executive assistant Joan McCarthy picked it up, gave the answer she had been told to give, put down the receiver, picked it right up again.

"What's the buzz?" Nick Green asked HR/PR.

Bambi Cartwright checked Twitter and Facebook on her phone, shook her head.

"Not much."

"Not much?"

"Nothing."

The shooting was just something they tried every year to gain publicity, interest for the release of the latest Sophomore History textbook.

It had worked at first, but was now perfunctory. Nobody goes for it. This one was supposed to depict like John Wilkes Booth or some shit, Nick thought he recalled.

"Who knows! Does it freeking matter?"

Was the way Nick explained the idea to the department managers years ago when they asked who the dead person was supposed to be.

"Everybody leads with blood. Watch the news. Read the books, the papers. It's blood or it's a dud. Dude."

The magazine and the latest in-house numbers said that publishing is dead.

"How come nobody told me! Did anyone think to let me know this fairly interesting news?"

He ripped off his cap and flipped it, expertly, as if planned, onto one of the giant antlers on Big Gus.

He did not shoot it, he told anyone new to the office. Either his father or grandfather, or it was there when they moved in, or it was given to them. Some stupid schmucking legend said the head showed up one day on the front sidewalk and the receptionist of that era held the door open with her foot and dragged it inside.

It could be true.

It did not matter now.

Could they even put out this new edition, which was supposed to be ready yesterday? Should they? Or should they just shut it down, go home, go fishing. Shoot themselves.

Nikostatos Greenberg was the latest of the Greenbergs to run "Beantree Barkham Bangor ... Kruszynianys Publishing, Inc."

And he wasn't going to be the last, not going to be the one who let it run into the ground. He had nine children and perhaps one, two of them qualified, still on the hook, within reach at home, if not fully committed, yet, to taking over the family business.

The New Fife publishing house was the only real remaining business in New Town. If it went down, so did the town, the people.

Nick Green had lived here all his life. He was not moving. If he ruined the business and the town, he would have no fun the rest of his life. His neighbors would stare at him, at the gas station, at church, at the ballgame.

Just stare. They would never say anything, but they would stare.

There would be no ballgames, the school would close.

He wanted to have some fun.

He deserved to have some fun.

He wanted to quit. He wanted to go fishing. But he did not want to fail, to have to think about this for the rest of his life.

He wanted to think about fish and smell like fish.

Ahh, that would be perfect.

CHAPTER TWO

"If you tell the truth, you don't have to remember anything."
— *Mark Twain*

The ambulance yanked and rolled and banged into the hospital emergency bay.

The driver rammed it into park while his partner was already climbing into the box.

The bag rolled back and forth on the floor, hitting the metal locker one side and then the other.

The driver threw open the back doors.

Now both emergency workers wrestled with the body bag, trying to pin it down like a bowl of black Jello.

They pressed with one hand while both searched for the zipper with the other.

The body made noises, huffing and grumbling.

They got the head out.

The man stood straight up, his balding skull rubbing the top of the metal box.

He shed the plastic garbage bag while making sure the driver and helper saw his red, sweaty angry face.

"What the hell!" he said.

"Sorry, there were some bumps," said the driver as the helper leaned to pick up and tidy.

"Hey, wait a minute, can I get a photo?"

"Just a sec," said one of the EMTs.

"Wait!"

"Okay, shoot," said the driver guy EMT.

A flash fired. For a split-moment the ambulance lit up, freezing the surprised faces forever.

Their eyes cleared and they saw the man with the camera and the pen between fingers.

First they lunged with their arms and then began to move their feet while keeping their heads down, leaping out onto the concrete as the door to the street banged closed.

They stopped.

"We done?" said one of the three men.

"Yep, that should do it," said another.

"Good," said the third.

As the department heads filed silently out of the office, Nikostatos Greenberg stood underneath the bull moose head at his window looking over the Beantree Barkham Bangor ... Kruszynianys campus.

He saw years, months, a day.

He saw himself holding the hand of his father looking out at the river, fishing poles in their hands and a coffee can of worms. Behind them someone came running and his father excused himself again to Niko to return to the office, leaving Niko to drag back the dry poles and worms.

He saw an ancient maroon brick building standing square and strong and around it popping up a gym from the ground, and many all-glass buildings, a daycare with playground. He saw a pasture turn into a parking lot, a sawmill, smokestacks, rolling lawns and a nine-hole Par 3 course.

In his mind's eye he saw the statue on the front lawn, the old guy in the suit who looked like nobody Nick had ever seen or heard of, right by, too close actually, to the electrical "3B 1K" sign and marquee with the current sub-title.

In the glass buildings Niko saw the town's reflection, the convenience store that had been the neighborhood grocery, the furniture store that had been going out of business for ten years, and the all you can eat "if you care to" Chinese restaurant.

All based on the Sophomore American History textbook. That's what his great-grandfather had concentrated on, done everything in his power to grab.

"This is it, the big one," he said.

"Whoever controls the past controls the present ... and the future ... and stuff like that."

That was actually carved in the side of a big tree in Nick's backyard, way up, the second or third branch.

That slogan was also in cursive on the marquee at the big cloverleaf entrance and on the paychecks and the employee parking permits.

"This Is it."

Now, according to not only this recent study in *Book Publishing Right Now*, but other studies that he knew of, yet to be released, the interest in sophomore history was perhaps not what it used to be.

For years students had thought it irrelevant, and now teachers, administrators and school boards were beginning to catch the drift.

"But History does not stop! What the hell!"

Nick threw up his hands and turned from the window, reached up as high as he could, jumped, climbed up on the rolling chair, then to the desk, grabbed the Yankees cap from the antler.

It was time to meet with his generals.

Nick Green walked fast, quickly, many steps quickly, it took so many steps for him to get anywhere.

He didn't care.

He didn't have a care in the world, is how he liked to play it, and so he swung his arms wide and smiled and stuck his chin up, exposing to the world his sweaty neck stubble.

He walked along the winding sidewalk, the intimate landscaping of trees, bushes, little ponds.

He marched through each of the buildings, front door to back, saying hello to the receptionists and everyone he saw, at times going a step and a half out of his way, shaking hands.

He stopped in The Hall of History, where every textbook the company had ever published was displayed in dusty trophy cases on both sides.

He wanted his son or daughter or somebody to be able to keep walking through these buildings and stopping to look and not being able to see to the end, just like his father had before him and way back.

Nick ground his teeth, narrowed his eyes, shook his head, pivoted and kept going, pushing it even a little faster.

He came to The Big Warehouse, pulled hard on the thick wooden doors, stepped inside and hopped back just as a forklift zipped past.

"Beep-beep!"

Nick raised his chin to nod to Eddie talking to some guy over at the counter and kept walking.

Eddie followed.

They walked together through the warehouse with the hundred feet ceilings and rows of boxes and pallets and sawdust.

Together Nick and Eddie marched together in silence out the thick grey double doors out onto the rolling green campus, inside other buildings, some humming like a modern day glass beehive, others dark, damp as a dungeon, like the Piper, picking up others along the way.

Nick and Eddie led the group finally down a moist, winding iron staircase to a wet, oily brick floor and stood together, at the bottom of the publishing ocean, amid a pod of fifty-feet-high boilers.

They talked to each other, a bit, but could not hear, and gave up. They smelled creosote, heard rumbling and roaring, dripping, a tropical rainforest after dark.

They looked for lions leaping.

They waited.

Way down on the other end came a sloshing sound, louder, louder.

A tall, skinny man, his hands stuck inside the pockets of stained grey coveralls, appeared through the steam and humidity, not bothering to pick up his feet, running his overshoes through the puddles that were everywhere.

He nodded briskly to Nick, Eddie, hustled through the group, and led them to the break room.

They crowded inside the grey brick room, finding space on the oil-stained ragged sofa, metal chairs.

Eddie grabbed the one big comfortable chair, oil-stained, springs showing.

Just as always somebody tried a penny in an ancient gumball machine.

The tall, skinny man, Artie, flicked off the radio, shut the door and made coffee.

Nick hoisted himself to a metal barstool, drew a deep breath and began to explain the situation.

He made eye-contact, looked around seriously at the group: Artie, Eddie, Jose, Willie, Roy, Juanita, Fred, Clarence, Earl, Manuel, Rita, Ray, Marvin, Floyd.

They came from maintenance, typesetting, margins & spacing, fonts, cover art, sales, glue, trimming, sawmill, paper, offset.

Everyone smoked cigarettes but Nick and Clarence.

Nick smoked a cigar.

Clarence spit Skoal Wintergreen into a Styrofoam cup stamped with oil fingerprints.

They took the white half-full Styrofoam cups from Artie, threw them back, held them up for more.

Artie found butterscotch cookies and flung them around the room, caught like frogs with flies.

Nick told them how this was the season for the release of the new sophomore history textbook to the high schools of the nation.

They had been working on it since this time last year after the release of the last textbook.

Not every high school got a new textbook every year. The teachers and administrators argued that history does not change. They don't need to purchase new books every year, or even every other year. Nick's sales team argued back that there is always new history, new things being discovered, new things to add, worksheets, study guides, and you don't want your students, who could also go to the high school next door if they wanted, to think they are getting screwed out of any history, do you?

But times were tight.

Sometimes The Big Pitch did not work.

And sometimes, maybe every twenty years or so, someone gets the idea that history is not important. We can live with these books for another five or ten years and besides, it's boring. Our parents don't care about it. The kids sure don't. And even the history teachers are starting to think maybe something more relevant to the lives of the students, bird calls or face painting, would be Benjamins better spent.

"You just need to promo it a bit, more," said Juanita, crossing her legs and biting a cookie.

"Advertising and hype works for movies and pop. You just need some ideas, Niko," said Floyd.

"What can you do?" said Roy.

"Cancel the new season?"

"We have orders," said Nick. "Not many, a few. And we have a book. Everyone's worked the whole year on this. We're on schedule. We're ready, but for some reason, the whole history zeitgeist just exploded in our goddamn faces.

"How was the shoot?" said Jose.

"Any luck?" said Willie.

"Nah," said Nick.

"They done figured it out."

"How about we put out a leak there's a big mistake, a gaffe in the book?" said Rita.

"That'll get people's attention. Something big and then go ahead and say we're going to fix it, but the main thing is, it gets people talking about sophomore history again in the coffee shops and board rooms."

Nick pointed at Rita with a cigar.

"That's good. I like it.

"What else, guys? C'mon, c'mon."

"Make it more interesting," said Marvin, crunching his cup and firing it way short of a full trash can.

"Like how?" said Nick.

"Like how?" said Marvin.

"How do I know like how? History is some boring shit."

"Make it more meaningful, to the kids," said Clarence from the far end of the sofa, pushing a spring down into the arm.

"Narrative, the story," said Artie, looking back over his shoulder from the coffee creamers.

"Wolfe, Breslin, new journalism," mumbled Juanita.

Artie snapped his fingers at her and winked.

"Make it truthful," said Earl.

"Truthful?" said Nick.

"It's schmuckin' truthful already, whatdya mean truthful? Like how?"

"Not rea ...," both Manuel and Ray started at the same time.

Ray nodded to Manuel to go ahead.

"Not really," he said.

"There's a lot in there that ain't the, ya know, totally on the whole up and up."

"Ha!"

Nick puffed and squinted and spoke through the smoke.

"Tell that to Max Karp.

"Of course, it's the truth. It's history. History's history. Boom-de-deboppa-deboom!"

He bit the cigar and swiveled to pound the counter.

Everyone shook their heads and looked at the floor or the cookie in their hand or the cigarette in their hand or their empty coffee cup.

"Make up some shit," said Eddie.

Nick saw Eddie was doodling and walked over to see. Eddie covered it with his arm as he looked up at Nick.

Eddie put up both hands.

"Just sayin'.

"War-a da Worlds. You know what ah'm talkin' about. They love that shit.

"Aaannd, if it's in a hist'ry book, you know ... it's hist'ry. What can I say?"

CHAPTER THREE

"The reason I talk to myself is because I'm the only one whose answers I accept."

— George Carlin

The radio on the counter crackled and talked about the story in the paper about the murder on the front lawn on Ninth Street.

"What'd they say?" said Nick, pointing at the radio with toast.

"You got a cover?"

Nick's wife asked him as she set out the green beans on a red hot pad.

"Course we got a cover."

Nick brushed the heads of three children on his way to the door and the front porch. He paused at the top step as he always did to see that the smoke of the factory was straight, the correct color and the correct volume.

Ever since the fire of 1975.

He stood with his father right there on the steps, holding their fishing poles, checking the smokestacks, looking for black, not the boring white, no wind, same old thing.

Nick remembered the glorious black smoke, like tires burning, and the smell like old tomato soup, and how his father handed him his pole and ran as if people were on fire, which they were, to his father, the people living inside those precious history books.

He recalled his own thoughts: burn it down and go fishing, get up on the big grader and drive the grader himself and push the rubble back to make room on the shore.

Nick opened the glass door of the cover design office not without trepidation.

He eased himself inside with one long silent step and another quick one-two.

He saw the blonde back of Lori Groome's head and imagined kissing it, Groome, the art department head, as she stared at a computer screen in the middle of a horseshoe of computers with all sizes of screens, with the chairs vacated in various modes of escape, stealthy to fast.

The walls were decorated in sophomoric history book art, some award plaques, a few newspaper clippings memorialized behind glass.

He got closer and saw how intent she was in her reflection in her screen.

She mumbled, moved her nose closer to the glass.

She was impressive in looks and intensity.

If he wasn't married. If he was a hundred years younger, a foot taller. If he had shaved today, this week, who knows?

Nick tiptoed around a chair and purse.

He was close.

If he was an assassin he would have her or spare her. He was that schmuckinggoddamned close.

He stood behind her and heard the Chinese menu mumbling.

She clicked, fumbled in her purse at her feet for her card, returned the card, stopped in motion, looked back at him and ...

"Ye-eess?" she said, annoyed.

"The Easter Bunny," he said.

She saw it was him, turned back to her computer, clicked on "white plastic spork" rather than "chop sticks."

Nick sat in a grey padded chair on wheels three spots down the line.

He hummed the tune from the radio news show as he touched the personal items on the desk in front of him as if deciding whether to buy.

He covered the robin's egg blue mouse with his hand, hiding it.

He moved it back and forth, sideways, trying to make the cursor on the screen go where he wanted.

"So, Nicky, what's up?"

"Can you show me the cover? I mean, I know what it is, I know, but, can we talk about it?"

She turned toward him.

"As in?"

"Just put it on your screen, ya know, however you ..."

He kicked two chairs out of the way and dragged himself up to her.

She turned to her screen.
Their knees touched.
"Oh, sorry," she said.
There it was.

AMERICAN HISTORY 101
Triumph of The American Nation

"How many times we used that?" he asked, putting a fat finger on the screen.
"It's been awhile," she said.
"Why?"
He shook his head and said nothing.
He looked intently at the front cover, the square photos of Jefferson, Washington, Lincoln, a teacher's desk, a flag, an artsy foggy apple on the desk.
The back cover showed a desert camouflage military uniform over flag, with some quotes.
"What are are options?" he said.
"Well, we've got Andrew Jackson, but nobody knows who he is, Lewis & Clark, maybe Sakajawee, ya know, but that's just asking for trouble. She's pointing at something, but what, exactly?"
"Right," said Nick.
"You're right. We don't need no trouble."
He pushed away from the desk with his hands and his feet in the air as if it were an Olympic sport now.
"We might need to do something," he said.
"Change it up a bit, you know."
She swiveled to watch him.
She stood, hands on hips, mouth open.
He could see her in the door glass.
"What!"
He heard her just as the door closed.

CHAPTER FOUR

"Art is the lie that enables us to realize the truth."
— *Pablo Picasso*

Nick scuffled on the sidewalk by the street, paralleling the river on the far side of the campus and the stream of cars running right next to him.

The sub-title bunker had been his great-grandfather's big deal.

In the spirit of the Cold War and personal bunkers in suburban homes being the thing, he had come up with the idea of making the sub-title of the sophomore history book top secret, hoping to increase its import by secrecy and showboating.

Nickostatos Greenberg No. 1 had sat in The Garamond Bar downtown and written it all out on a napkin as the legend went as written by himself.

He had decided that the unveiling of the sophomore history textbook sub-title would be Top Secret, developed and hidden and protected, and launched, from a bunker in the middle of the giant lawn on the campus.

And because it was a Big Secret it would be a Big Deal.

And the Big Deal would be connected right to The Pageant, the local book launch and the national coverage, just like they paraded the goddamn gopher and his shadow, they would cover the new national sophomore history textbook to be placed in every classroom in America.

It worked. Pretty good. At times.

Until now.

Now the whole goddamn shebang had fallen apart. On Nick's watch.

There was no way to get to The Sub-Title Bunker.

The idea that management liked to put out, even though everyone knew it was bullshit, was that if you were ready to enter The Sub-Title Bunker it would make itself available to you. Kind of like the waitresses at The Times New-Roman when a kid turned 21.

Unless you had a schmucking key.

Nick headed out over the lawn, angling toward the launch site.

He found the red key fairly easily on his Captain Kangaroo ring on his belt, unlocked the padlock, pushed the gate open just far enough, locked the lock.

He walked over the rocky, bumpy lawn. It didn't get the care the rest of the rolling lawns received as some of the "commanders" in the bunker were reluctant to allow the grounds crew access.

Nick heard the cameras focusing, whirring, swiveling, following him.

He slid his hand down the railing and trotted down the cement steps into the ground, like a team into a locker room under the field, he sometimes imagined, not today, today he had other shit on his mind.

He opened the heavy grey door that should have been locked.

Nick stepped into the concrete block room, large, dark, lit by three rows of computer screens.

He heard the ballgame on a radio somewhere.

He clomped down an empty aisle, grabbing half a sandwich from a keyboard, around an empty chair obstacle course. Cigarettes smoked alone in orange and green glass ashtrays.

There they all were, eating sandwiches and smoking inside The Launch Room.

Nick smiled, shook his head and entered another grey door into the glassed room where everyone gathered around two men playing chess on their computer screens.

The two computers sat just far enough away from each other that one man could not operate both.

The Fail-Safe launch method had started out as a lark, but now was factual.

This glassed room had its own oxygen, water, septic, security system, with real cyanide pills and .45 pistols to kill the other guy if you think he has gone mad.

Nick waved his hand at the smoke.

One guy took dollar bill bets in the corner.

They all watched in silence as the two men at the computers, strapped in by shoulder harnesses on the launch chairs did battle.

Nick handed the man three thin bills and nodded at the guy on the right.

He sat on the metal window sill and put his feet up on the black steel launch code box marked "Ibid."

He waited, waited, until one guy won and the guy in the corner started taking and handing out money. Nick joined the line in heading out the door. It was hot in there. He swiped sweat off his forehead with the wet back of his hairy hand.

He waited for Deanno, one of the chess combatants.

They walked into the first glassed office on the left, leaving the door open.

Deanno sat at the desk.

Nick stood, then sat in the one chair, then stood.

"I should know better'n bet against you," said Nick.

"What's up, boss?" said Deanno.

"What's ya got for this year?" said Nick.

"I thought you knew," said Deanno.

"I do. I did. Just tell me again, huh?"

Deanno worked his computer. Nick looked around the office at the plaques commemorating the sub-titles of past years.

The American Pageant. Triumph of the Americn Nation. Misspelled, what a schmucking deal that was. The Great Republic. Land of Promise.

"Oh, yeah.

"Here ya go."

Deanno swiveled the screen so Nick could see.

Nick looked quick.

"Yep.

"When do you launch?" he said.

"When is the pageant?" asked Deanno.

"I gotta talk ta her 'bout that," said Nick.

"Well," said Deanno, leaning back in his chair, putting his feet on his desk, getting ready for something coming.

"Then it would be about a week before that. Give us some time to boot up, all that, you know how it goes."

"Oh," said Deanno, putting his feet down and picking up two baseball gloves from his desk.

He tossed one to Nick.

"It's just a thing," said Deanno, "but, you know, you know how it goes."

Deanno put the glove up around his face to talk.

As did Nick.

"Yeah, I know," said through the webbing of the glove.

"Can't be too careful," said Deanno.

"Huh? Oh, yeah, yeah, you're right there."

Nick liked the smell of the glove, the leather like summer. He and his father had talked through the gloves when they sat on the porch steps some times. His father didn't want any competitor driving past and getting an advantage, and then he made the launch team use 'em whenever anyone talked to anyone else in the bunker, because you never knew who was a spy and who wasn't, ya know?

"We might have to," began Nick.

He reached out and kicked the door closed, keeping the glove at his face, looking over the top of the fingers at Deanno who sat again with his feet on the desk, making his expensive schmucking chair lean way back, holding the glove to his face with his right hand even though it was the wrong hand and trying to work his computer mouse with the other.

It wasn't easy.

"Change things up a little bit," said Nick.

"What's that?" said Deanno, not really looking at Nick.

Nick leaned forward in his chair.

"We need a new schmucking sub-title! Shithead! You hear me now?"

Deanno slowly finished what he was doing and took his time looking back at Nick, who had sat back in his chair, his face and neck blazing, his eyes glaring wide as full moons with spy cameras and eyebrows on Full-Schmucking-Focus.

"Why is that?" said Deanno.

"It's all set, same Saturday in May, or June, usually, unless someone has a hair thing and has to change the launch date."

He slammed his boots to the cement.

"Change what, Nicky?" he whispered through the Rawlings fingers.

"I don't know," said Nick.

"Sumptin' diffrunt, that's all. That's all I know. Sumptin' diffrunt."

Deanno reached inside a drawer in his desk, pulled out a manila file, opened it, slid one sheet away where Nick couldn't see it and handed the next one to Nick.

"It's some possibles," said Deanno.

"Our possibles file, you know."

"Awright," said Nick, beginning to take a look.

He scanned down the page with the heading "Posibles."

Hard Working Americans

White Picket Fences

What's For Dinner?

What Is Your Favorite Color

If You Were A Tree

If You Were A Lunch Bucket

Nick threw the paper back at the desk. It fluttered to the cement floor.

"What's that shit?" he said.

"What's for dinner? If you were a lunch bucket. Are ... you ... schmucking ... kidding me?"

He let the glove sit on his seat as he got up.

He accepted a stick of gum from Deanno and turned toward the door.

"We need to change them," said Nick.

"It. Change it," said Deanno grabbing his glove again quick, not quite getting it to his face in time.

"I don't know what," said Nick, inching out the door.

"I'll tell you what, just as soon as I know what. Okay?"

He stuck his nose inside the door just as it closed.

"Yeah, okay," said Deanno, pressing his nose flat into the pocket of the glove that smelled like summer and grass and sun and glove oil and plenty of good stuff.

CHAPTER FIVE

"The most important kind of freedom is to be what you really are. You trade in your reality for a role. You trade in your sense for an act. You give up your ability to feel, and in exchange, put on a mask. There can't be any large-scale revolution until there's a personal revolution, on an individual level. It's got to happen inside first."

— *Jim Morrison*

Nick paused at the top of the outside steps with his hand on the railing, catching his breath, taking time that he never took, to look over the campus, the town, the river, his house over there on the hill.

This has to work. He has to save the company. He won't be the one to fail.

Or not.

Maybe he will be the one to fail.

Who's to stop him?

He could fall flat on his face and not have the gumption to put out his hands, as his father had said.

He walked back over the interior lawn in z-style, back and forth, to be able to safely pass over the minefield that his father had liked people to think about.

He padlocked the gate, tested it.

No. He would be the one who would boost pre-orders. That's who he was.

The Commies Are Coming The Commies Are Coming.

The Terrorists Are Coming.

The Criminals Are Coming.

He mumbled to himself to test how they sounded.

"Big Bees!" he said out loud just as he turned and saw Honey White Bear-de la Rosa.

She stood tall and straight, deep black hair practically everywhere, high cheekbones, spotless white peasant dress, black high heels, gold rings and bracelets about all over.

She stood on the sidewalk watching him walking toward her like in a Pepsodent or DentuCream commercial. She turned her hips slightly to accent her leg, with her bag over her shoulder.

She wore her long black hair in a bun.

Her makeup hid what she wanted hid.

"Walk weeth meee Neeckolahs," she said.

Nick stared into her chest and nodded.

As they turned up the sidewalk, Nick got a thought.

"Have the kids write it. It's supposed to be third-grade level or some shit. And 'dem stupid schmuckin' sophomores should be able to unnerstan' at least that shit."

She walked like the Sunday racehorse past the stands.

"Keep up, Neeckolas," he heard her growl and put his head down to catch on up.

CHAPTER SIX

"If you want to tell people the truth, make them laugh, otherwise they'll kill you."
   — Oscar Wilde, *"The Nightingale and the Rose"*

"So, Neecky."

He followed her past a silent sentry receptionist to her office where she began checking things on the desk.

She nodded at a chair and he sat.

Nick had long been in awe of the black-haired widow realtor. She was an old friend of his father's and based on looks from his mother when her name came up, maybe a close friend.

The office was also the headquarters for the local historical society based on her possession of the bone dust of one Nickostatos Greenberg The Very 1st who went and got himself lost in a Hearts game in the back rooms of The Garamond to Amos White Bear and now there they were, on display in White Bear-De la Rosa Realty.

She made mumbly small-talk noises while standing over her desk checking her notes.

Nick scanned the walls again. There was no radio, no windows, no magazines. Nothing but the fog of kiwi-strawberry perfume. He strained to see her plaque as President of The Daughters Of The Last Century in the middle of twenty such gold plaques behind her.

The next wall showed twenty photos of her with Nick's great grandfather, his father and he at the start of the Parade that led to the band shell and The Pageant.

And there were her church photos, baptisms, confirmations. Nick thought he was smart enough not to mention religion with Honey, but he was not sure anymore. He wanted to tell her what he really thought of all those "nice little stories," the gospels, that some guy just made up, prob'ly, to impress a girl.

She knows, he thought.

"I know, Neeckolas."

She sat like a cheetah in tall grass and folded her hands on the desk.

Well, then, here we go, he thought, and leaned forward, mouth open.

"Thee pressure you are undrrr.

"Thee new book, your wife, your cheeldren, the ungrateful department managers, too much for one little man, I know, darling."

"Nah," said Nick.

"I got it, it's not like that," he said, while thinking, what managers?

"How can I help you? I want to help."

He stared into her eyes, brown, like birds in a grove of hoop earrings and feathers and bracelets and rings.

"The Pageant, of course."

She sat back, scowled over Nick's shoulder and subtly nodded her head to make someone in the doorway go away for now, come back later, I love you.

"I have an idea," she said.

"About a new place to put The Sales Team Dunk Tank."

She got up and began to pace behind her desk like Kennedy during the missile crisis thing.

"It's always by the toilets," said Nick.

"It's wearing the grass away," she said.

"Someone complained and I absolutely agree!"

She stretched her arms toward the ceiling.

"It needs to be moved somewhere else. If not, the whole thing is ruined.

"The world will end, Neeky," she leaned forward, showing her bosom and hummed."

"Listen, Honey," he said.

"Boom," she said as she stood and shot up her hands again and made Nick bounce in his chair.

"See. 'dat's da t'ing. I got to talk to you."

She stopped in the far corner of the room, turned and folded her arms across her chest, now guarding her breasts. He imagined her strong muscles like conveyer belts stretching and pressing her undergarments into a rock-hard ball.

He stood and folded his hands at his waist.

"See. The books. They ain't sellin'. We got no pre-orders. If they don't sell, we don't drink. No beer, no vodka. No Gatorade."

"We don't eat, you mean, I'm sure. None?" she said.

"No. Not none for exact. Just not that many, see?"

He moved two steps toward her.

She backed up, fear in her eyes as her hands clutched her clothing. He stopped.

"So. I think we need to change some things. Like in your pageant."

She drew a deep breath, gathered herself to charge and rushed past him, brushing his shoulder, into the outer office.

He heard her crying somewhere.

He heard "not MY pageant!" "Theee worldzz pageant!"

Nick waited for a while, until he heard nothing, then he reached to grab one of the red-striped mints from the glass bowl just as the receptionist moved it just far enough away.

Nick removed his cap, part-way to nod to the receptionist on his way out.

CHAPTER SEVEN

Make up some shit.

Not a bad idea. Not great, but how many great ideas were there left? Not bad is the new pyramids.

That's what Nick was thinking as he walked from the realty office through downtown.

He could ask the writers in his History Department to do it, but that would be trouble. He'd have to do a bunch of pushing and there was no time for that whole big production again.

He passed The Baskerville, slowed, looked, kept going.

They all did the job, those history types, but each had their own subtle style, nuance, constituency. They were schmucking weirdos.

He needed to go to the schools. He knew this one teacher.

Nick turned the corner, up the hill.

He leaned into it, his hand rubbing the brick building.

He walked with his head down, stopped, looked up, all around, and remembered that's the way his father used to walk, and it made him so mad, he came up with all these metaphors in his mind for what his father looked like when he did that and now all he could think of was that it was a good way to catch your breath and see you are not swerving.

The one hand on the rough, old brick also helped, a string line to ensure uniformity of direction.

During one of his breath-look-around stops up the hill Nick wondered, why should he care.

He should just go fishing. His grandfather never went fishing. Never. And his father never went. They passed it down. Now Nick was not going fishing. And his children had never been fishing.

They had been everywhere else. They did everything else until their goddamned brains fell out.

Nobody reads.

Who gives a good-goddamn these days about a damn history book. It's not a movie. It's not on TV. It's not the purple phone in your hands.

Washington? Lincoln. God-damn Jefferson? Who gives a shit about these guys in their white hair and their moles and their big statues on the quarters? Huh? Who. Tell me one guy, Lord, tell me one guy.

Nick pushed up hard up the hill, feeling the sun on his neck and the sweat in his underwear.

He ran out of building and angled toward the center of the sidewalk.

The alley gave a good reason to stop and look all around.

He looked around.

He put his head down and took one step into the gravel when out of his side vision came the familiar sight of the Pontiac front quarter panel, faded green and rusting in the dent hollow in the shape of his thigh of thirty years ago, where the front quarter panel had hit him after a softball game. Someone had not called another player off or the other player had not yelled "I got it" as they perhaps should have and afterwards after coming out of an establishment in this very neighborhood had perhaps not stopped when someone else had been walking and there was the dent, still there. Right there.

"Who controls the present controls the past."

At the sound of the gravel whiskey whisper Nick planted his red tennis shoes in a fresh pile of pigeon mess and formed his hand into an arthritic fist and stopped in time.

The old faded lemon-lime Pontiac rumbled and squeaked like the factory on the last day up to place the driver face to face.

With the sun in his eyes Nick could not so much see the face as smell the cigarette smoke and the dog inside the car. He looked at the quarter panel to rest his eyes, the rusty cast of his right thigh. The long car with the wings used to be a classy olive famous on main street. The olive had spoiled.

"Who controls the present controls the past."

Goddamit! Like he didn't hear it already, so Kamil Kruszynianys thinks he has to repeat it.

"Or something like that."

Nick said what he was supposed to say to complete their old saw.

The NPR announcer in the dash gave the details of the life of Tchaikowsky as if nobody knew.

"Henry Foorrd," Kamil growl-whispered like a Corleone and Nick waved his short arms and pudgy hands in front of him like he was trying to swim in reverse.

"I don' wanna hear about Ford!" Nick said.

"His'try is bunk."

Kamil just kept comin'. Kept comin'."

"It's textbook season," said Kamil, stating the obvious in a way that he knew would drive Nick up the wall.

"Get one-a those?" said Nick.

He placed a hip on the car in a position that he was able to not look into the sun and now saw the dog in the back and the beer.

Kamil was Nick's best friend, he guessed.

They grew up together, went to most of high school, worked at the book factory on the line, digging ditches, footings, while their fathers watched from the office windows telling each other whose son was the best worker.

The Kruszynianys were there way before the Greenbergs, two weeks, three weeks, some in the families said a month.

Grandpa Kruszynianys started the book publishing company with Beantree, Barkham and Bangor. Took it over from them. They gambled. And ol' man Kruszynianys fished. And Grandpa Greenberg swore off fishing. No more.

He worked and worked and did nothing else and took over the company, waving his hands at Kruszynianys laughing, out there in the river, showing him a big bass.

The one thing old man Kruszynianys wanted before he died was to get the Kruszynianys name a little higher up, and delete the ellipsis.

Old man Greenberg would never do it. Nick's father respected his father's wishes and never did it.

Kamil stuck his head out the window, handed Nick the cigarette and spit on Nick's shoes.

Nick knew he had to do it.

Most of the time he missed or it was a spray that went nowhere or he tried to miss.

The vendetta.

"You wan' a ride?" said Kamil.

Nick looked up the hill and down at the car interior, the springs, the stains, the spills, the dog.

"Nah, s'okay, just goin' to the school."

"You got a late assignment?" Kamil smiled, showing where he might be able to use a tooth.

"Yeah, yeah," said Nick, flicking the cigarette over the car into the alley, shooing the ol' Pontiac like the last doggie out of the corral.

"Get-ahta-here!"

CHAPTER EIGHT

"Never be afraid to raise your voice for honesty and truth and compassion against injustice and lying and greed. If people all over the world ... would do this, it would change the earth."

— *William Faulkner*

Finally he arrived at the summit, the flat area of town, and he smelled the burning leaves, heard the children playing, felt the apple pie breeze on his cheek.

Nick stopped at the four-way and stood as drivers stopped, looked at him, kept going, others stopped, waited for him to cross, gunned it through the intersection.

Nick stood with his hands in his pockets, staring at the big brick school where his one daughter taught sophomore American History, 101.

And over on the apple pie side of the street, another daughter played with her home-school children in the front yard, tossing a ball.

Why couldn't he just quit.

Keeping his hands in his pockets he shuffled his feet around like Charlie Chaplin to survey down that direction.

He's old. He's been at this for a long time. But never before like this, not with The Sophomore History Textbook Debacle that would follow him around in his mind forever wherever he went, fishing, to get beans, to the ballgame, to The Memorial Cemetery up behind City Hall.

He needed something new, something big, something that people would see and say, yes, that's interesting, and tell others and then

Nick could wave as he walked out the door of his big, hugely successful retirement party and head right for an old fishing boat and perhaps disappear over the horizon.

Triumph of the Blah-blah-blah Nation.

Make up some shit.

He shuffled another ninety degrees and smiled. Somebody he knew waved and Nick stuck up his chin.

He shuffled again and saw young people driving with their heads down working their phones.

People do not read.

Washington, Lincoln, Jefferson?

Are you kidding me?

They should put a rock star, a football player, a famous chef on the cover. That actually might work.

Hmm.

Go supersize or go home.

The Paranormal Pageant.

The Reptilian Republic.

Land of Greed.

My Big Fat Country.

Nick waved to a woman his age who was stopping for him, then stepped into the street when he was sure.

He ducked his head to walk, which made it easy to hit the opposite curb perfectly and not stumble.

He stopped at the intersections of the sidewalks.

He waved at the school, at the window up on the third floor with his daughter now hanging out.

"Hey, Papa!"

The home-school daughter now also saw him.

He waved with both hands.

He gulped a deep breath as if it were gold and so it choked him. He leaned over and grabbed his knees, causing his daughters to lean farther out the window and brush hands down the apron and put one hand on the gate.

He raised up and waved again, both hands, I'm all right.

Like Kennedy he needed to make peace with the Rooskies. He needed to go against old guard. Make the world new. It would not be easy, but it must be done, even if it killed him. It must be done.

He crossed kitty-corner over the street without looking, causing a pickup to stop quick. Nick smiled, put up a hand like the mayor in the pageant parade, headed for the school building.

Out of the corner of his eye he watched the home-school daughter watching him with hands on hips as he fast-walked over the school front lawn, head down, fists tight and pumping.

He kicked through the plastic soda containers and cigarette packs surrounding the statue that was a replica of the one right in front of the publishing house main office that looked a little like it was trying to hide the marquee and sign.

He entered the old school, as if entering a Jimmy Breslin column, a cathedral, sacred space.

Where he went three times a week religiously until his sophomore year.

A door slammed a block away.

Someone laughed loud on a distant floor.

Nick stood like a rabbit whose one weapon is stillness. His nose wiggled and brought back hamburgers and strawberry drink. His ears stretched to catch the direction of inherent danger.

Over there.

The principal's office.

Nick saw a hand on the corner wall and headed up the shined, painted grey cement steps to the upper classmen areas he had never seen.

Up, up, around, around, sliding his hand on the shined, painted grey smooth rail.

He heard authoritative, nit-picky, fussy, critical, nagging steps behind him and closing in. He leaned forward to climb faster, swiped off his Yankees cap and wiped his forehead with his arm.

He stopped and looked up.

There.

She was.

The girl of his dreams.

Nice everything.

Long everything, everything smooth.

He gripped the shiny railing as if one hand was enough to keep him from falling off the face of the earth.

She took the middle of the steps, smiling at him, commanding each shined step as if it were her own, while bluebirds and bees fluttered all about her making sure everything was just so, finding they had nothing to do.

She stopped on the same step.

They looked into each other's eyes and somewhere somebody played Neil Diamond, Simon and Garfunkel, Four of Bread's Greatest Hits, and The Carpenters.

Her concern was legit.

She furrowed her brow, moved in closer, gently took Nick's arm and asked if he was all right, if he needed help finding the door.

"Do you know where you are?" she said.

Behind him, around just a couple of turns, came the resolute steps.

Nick nudged free of the teen angel and pulled himself up by the railing, up, up, around, around.

Nick arrived at the top floor.

This must be it.

He glanced around, snatched off his cap and peeked around again.

Nobody in sight, but the footsteps behind just kept coming like the posse on the trail of Sundance and Butch. Shoosh, whoosh, shoosh.

He flattened his back and arms against the lockers and shuffled down the hall, grimacing at each locker handle in his back.

He came to the door, stuck his head around.

"Hello, Father."

He looked back, there she was, across the hall.

The steps behind him rounded the corner, and now more coming from the other end of the long, shiny hall.

The Principal Miss Bordeaux approached them, concerned with papers in her hands.

"Good morning, Mr. Greenberg," she said as she handed his daughter something and moved on, her shoes clicking.

She passed Sonny, the janitor headed this way. Sonny also worked part-time at the plant. Sonny was the shooter who always shot the actor in the opening scene shooting thing to begin Historical Days. Sometimes he dressed like Lee Oswald, sometimes James Earl Ray or Sirhan Sirhan or the guy who shot Reagan, once the woman who tried to murder Gerald Ford. But now, since Blaze Thornpine had actually been killed, how was Sonny not in jail then? Nick thought that he needed to check with The Big Shoot staff to ask what was going on with that.

"Hey, Mr. Nick," Sonny said, as he passed and also nodded to Nick's daughter.

"I think the coast is clear," she said, uncrossing her arms and turning sideways to welcome him over.

"Hey, Katie," he said.

"Uh, Mrs. Beantree."

She smiled again and quick waved him like a traffic cop with a pokey driver.

He pressed his cap into his stomach.

"Really?

He had never been in a sophomore history classroom.

"Yes," she said.

"It's about time, too."

He pushed his back into the side wall, the chalkboard, chalk tray, sending a ruler and a flag clattering to the floor.

He hurried to pick them up.

"Sorry," he said.

She helped him and gripped his arm.

"This is my father," she said to the class.

The students watched him. He watched them.

Katie led him to the front of the room and brought him a wooden barstool to perch, front and center.

"This is familiar," he mumbled.

"I'll listen," he said.

"You g'head, whatever you was doin', gowan."

"Well, actually," she said.

"Since I saw you coming across the lawn we have been waiting for you. It's new book time."

"Yes," he said.

"Well, maybe you could tell us about the new textbook, the new Sophomore History 101 text that your company will be producing, printing, in the very near future. It's a big deal. Most of this town has a connection, if not directly to the plant, then by way of children using the text and learning about America."

She hustled in and pinched his arm.

"And besides, we've got some extra time before lunch."

She stepped back and tossed out both arms.

"Nickostatos Greenberg, if you would not mind!"

She clapped with her hands stretched out long, and the children followed politely.

Katie grabbed the current book from her desk and handed it to her dad.

He held it in his lap, looked at the front cover, back cover, the photos of Washington, Lincoln, Jefferson, a teacher's desk, flag, repeating on the back, all on a red, white and blue background base.

"Well, yeah," he said.

He looked up and saw a full room, full faces all looking right at him.

"Stay on the same page," he said.

"Take it to the next level.

"I know, right?"

He ran his thumb quickly through the book, feathering all seven hundred and thirteen pages.

"What do you think?" he said.

"You like history?"

He smiled back at his daughter and waved a hand at her.

"Forget she's here."

"We were kind of hoping to hear about the new book," said Katie.

"Yeah-yeah."

He swiveled to her and then back.

"That's da thing, see?

"Somethin's not workin'.

"People aren't really reading these freakin' things."

"Sorry," he said over his shoulder without looking.

Nick saw in the classroom mostly white kids, but there were two that could be Mexican, he thought, and one black girl for sure, one Indian or Asian kid by the window.

"You read this book?" he turned to his daughter.

"Yes, we follow it, page by page, and the study guides and questions at the end of each chapter are very helpful. I was an advisor one summer to your writing department, Papa, if you recall."

"Yeah-yeah."

"You, you, you, you, you."

He pointed at the Mexican kids and the black kid and the Indian-Asian something kid.

"Stand up."

They looked at each other and slowly pushed themselves to the edge of their desks and glacially stood.

"You like this book?"

Two of the children shrugged their shoulders. One shook her head. One giggled, turning red behind her hand.

"Okay, sorry, you can sit."

He dropped the book flat on the floor and it banged.

The students jumped.

"That's the most excitement you ever got in this class, huh?" he said.

He looked at his daughter and she scowled back.

"Okay, I gotta go."

He climbed off his stool, pointed one gun-hand at his daughter and the other at the students.

"Stay on the same page, huh?"

Katie stayed standing by her desk, watching him, arms folded now across her chest as he went to the door."

He waved again with his cap, then entered the hallway, where he saw

Principal Miss Bordeaux standing with her back against a locker.

She walked with him as he moved past.

"It's not just here," she said.

"I'll be at the sales meeting, but we won't be ordering a new text," she said.

"It's just not worth it, I'm afraid. There's nothing new year to year. I mean history is history, right? And the cost, well, we need basketball uniforms for the girls. It's been seven years."

She silently walked with him to the third floor and said her goodbyes.

He walked round and round, his head up, looking at the black and white photos every now and then on the walls: Jefferson, Washington, Lincoln, a flag, a teacher's desk, an apple, now Washington again.

He stopped to sit on the statue and smoke his cigar, nodding at some kids hustling inside. He twisted the cigar out on the statue, stuck it into his coat pocket and walked over to see Janey, who he hadn't always gotten along with the greatest every single freeking time.

They always tried to do the big family thing with the big table and the big, happy talk, but it never worked that well that he could really remember.

As you might imagine in a family like the Greenbergs, history might be a big topic of conversation, but it wasn't. It was more that the business of publishing history textbooks for sophomores in high school was kept at arms length.

Janey always wanted to pull it in close.

Nick guessed he had not encouraged that.

He crossed the street, stepped up over the curb onto the terrace, swung open the squeaky front gate, bent to move a yellow plastic automobile from the sidewalk and left it. It was no use. The whole yard was scattered with primary colored plastic toys.

He stepped over the little car and made his way up the broken cement steps to the loose metal screen door.

He stepped into the front porch and saw a different story. It comprised a long, neat, tightly packed array of books and desks and tools for learning. Everything for the craft of education was on that long front porch, including beach balls, blocks, Legos, and red plastic sets of protractor, ruler and geometry triangle, arranged neatly, inside the plastic, everywhere.

Voices pulled him inside, and the smell of the apple pie, the hot, gooey fragrance of homemade apple stuff.

The little, cluttered kitchen steamed and smelled sweet and he wished someone would come in. This should be shared.

A light door slapped somewhere and running laughter brought him face to face with Janey, looking up at him, smiling, crushing her apron in her hands, her freckles pulsing with thought and action. Around her and behind gathered her children, his grandchildren.

If he could call one of them by name with a gun at his head he would do it right now.

He swiped his Yankees cap and pressed it to his stomach.

"Grandpa!"

They held out arms and moved closer, not quite touching, not quite speaking.

"Kinda dark in here."

He said as he looked around.

"We run energy efficient light bulbs," said one of the older girls.

"I saw you going over to the school. I didn't think we would see you," said Janey.

She wore her red hair in a long plait, big peasant hippie dress, no shoes, one gold tooth "for emergencies." All the kids had one, which was weird, but his wife had insisted. They got teased at school, but some day they may thank us, like that. They were still waiting.

"So."

He began counting heads with his eyes.

"Six," she said.

"You saw Able on the front porch. It's his reading time. He likes it out there."

"Nope," said Nick.

"Nobody out there."

"You just didn't see him," said Janey.

"If he was reading he didn't see you either."

"Hmmm," hummed Nick.

Janey had always been sort of a history dissident, he supposed was the polite way to put it.

At the Thanksgiving adult big table she complained that the others sent her to Siberia by rolling their eyes.

"Well," he said, picking up a shined stone with a hand-painted verse on it.

"This is nice."

Janey said something to the children, maybe in another language, and they all moved efficiently in different directions, to stations, to read, to sew, to paint, to wash dishes, to meditate, to exercise.

He watched them go.

"We're just beginning the next mod," Janey said.

"You came at a good time."

"I did?" he said.

"Nice."

"Would you like coffee?" she said, already moving toward the stone pot on the old wood stove, grabbing a log from the floor and pitching it inside, grabbing the vessel with a worn mitt.

"Yeah, can you smoke on the porch?"

They both sensed all the children stopping to listen.

She held the kettle still in the air to think.

"Sure," she said and poured them each a full cup from the uneven handmade mug set, each with names and sayings and dates painted on.

The children looked at each other as if they had just smelled "God Fart."

He headed for the porch and she followed with their mugs.

"The eyes are the key to the soul," she said as she sat on a wooden chair.

"The fingernails are the window to the heart."

Nick looked at his hands, torn, bloody stubs.

He made fists to hold his hot coffee and tried to smile.

"Well, there he is," he said, now noticing Able scrunched at the end of the porch.

Nick sat on the sofa, darting looks at the boy reading, immersed, with narrow eyes, brow furrowed, feet twitching, hand twirling his long hair.

Nick looked at the cover of the book and read the title out loud.

"Lies My Teachers Told Me."

He chuckled.

"That's you."

"No. Not me," said Janey.

"You're his teacher," he said.

"Oh, I get it.

"Lies. Like what lies. It's a joke book. I get it. You got me there."

"How old is ol' ..."

"Able is ten."

Nick counted out on his fingers.

"That would be ... fifth grade, huh?"

"Yes, if he were ..., still ... he reads at freshman college level. If that textbook would ever be in a "regular" (she made air quotes) high school classroom, it would be about sophomore level."

"Lies?" said Nick.

"What lies?"

Able dropped the book flat to make eye contact with Nick.

"There are so many," he said.

"So, even you teach history," Nick said to Janey.

"It's what he's interested in. It was really my idea, believe it or not."

"Stay on the same page," said Nick.

"Right? Take it to the next level. I know, right?"

Nick drank his coffee with his fists.

Janey adjusted something on her dress.

Able waited for Nick to speak.

Nick turned to Able.

"Well, I'll tell ya. My plan ... my plan is to change the book. You know, our book, the book. Right?"

Able nodded.

"Isn't it time, you know, for the new book?" said Janey. It's too late for that."

"We don't have any choice. That's what I told Honey White Bear."

"Oh, her," said Janey.

"I told her we got to change everything, that's what I'm thinking. We got to change the cover, change the insides, the pageant, the title, the sub-title."

"She said, it cannot be done, it should not be done, what would your grandfather and father have said?"

"I said, I don't schmucking know — sorry, sorry-sorry — but this is my call. I got to make the decision."

"It would impact everything," said Janey.

"Are you sure about this. It would change your whole business. It would affect your family, the whole town, the whole country perhaps."

"Prob'ly," said Nick.

"The whole world," said Able.

"I think you should."

"Have you asked Uncle Mick and Aunt Helen?" said Janey.

"Nope," said Nick.

"They're never around. Why should I?"

"Don't you think you should?"

"Nope."

He pulled the stub from his jacket pocket, dug in his pocket, scrounged in the other pocket.

"Here," said Able, sitting up, leaning forward, holding out a candle for Nick to light his cigar.

CHAPTER NINE

"If you look for truth, you may find comfort in the end; if you look for comfort you will not get either comfort or truth only soft soap and wishful thinking to begin, and in the end, despair."

— *C.S. Lewis*

Randy stood over the trays in the glow of the red light. The sports talk show hosts mumbled on low volume from the shelf.

He used the tongs to move the photo in the fix.

He held it up and smiled.

Randy hung the photo from a clothespin on the wire and went upstairs.

Randy was now "the promising new young editor" of the local weekly.

He had long questioned the publicity murders and fostered the conspiracy theories that swirled around that.

Nick called him a conspiracy kook, wouldn't have anything to do with the Wednesday Wingnut, as he called the Journal-Times.

And now Randy had him, had his tongs around Nick's nuts.

The black and white photo of the EMTs helping the man climb out of the body bag would run on page one tomorrow and probably the week after as well.

Randy sat in his office, his feet on his desk, his hands folded on his stomach, watching the foot and car traffic on main street out his window.

He reached to his desk for the sophomore history textbook that someone had brought in yesterday featuring a handwritten note on one of the first pages that the person had found suspicious, and knowing of Randy's proclivity toward suspicion, well, brought it in.

The note was in blue pen, printed, on the title page:

History Is So Boring.

Teachers just go throo the motions.

And then there was a drawing of a superhero firing laser beams or spider webs from its hands.

Pres'dents Book of Secrets

Platoz Cave.

Randy knew all about Plato's Cave and had written a number of editorials on the subject, so he didn't feel he could go there. The textbook writer in fact might very well have gotten the idea from him.

But the Presidents Book of Secrets, that was new.

Randy had inherited the newspaper from his wife, who had died in a very recent car accident. Randy had been a teacher, in the local schools, sophomore history.

This was his first go-round through the whole history festival cycle as the editor.

As a teacher he had used the textbook provided by Nick, just as everyone else did. But he didn't have to like it. He didn't like Nickostatos Greenberg, because of an old feud. Something his father had passed down about a dropped ball in the outfield during a softball game.

And so when he graduated college, got his dream job back at his old school and had to teach from Nick's book, well, he just hadn't considered how much it would bother him.

His wife ran the newspaper and he helped out, trying to nudge her toward the conspiracies that he saw as plain as the back of your hand. Sometimes he thought she knew more than she told him.

And then that strange, fateful night just as she was heading home from a long day at the paper she was run off the road by a carload of teenagers on their way out west for summer construction jobs who were never heard from again.

The office was decorated with Randy's collection of T-shirts and ball caps, hanging from walls, over the front of the counter, in the windows, bearing his favorite slogans:

The construction and maintenance of public myth

Conspiracy Theory — so dangerous we must outlaw it

Teacher — journalist — watchdog on power — that's their job — that's all we have

The only thing that can rescue society are real historians

The consensus hallucination that passes for reality

This photo is the thing that's going to break it all. They've always, for the past three-plus months, called him a nut.

But no more.

Randy got up, headed to his work desk. There was a change he needed to make in the masthead of the paper on the first inside page. He went to his computer.

The quote from Morris Berman made the masthead, with the official stuff about the paper, longer than it should be, but it was necessary, it was instructive.

"What people want is what they have always wanted, community, friendship, safety, sex, interesting things to think about ... and in return get crap — says here's a cellphone, here's lip gloss, here's television, channeled into substitute satisfaction ... generally people aren't satisfied with that, on some level."

Randy opened it, inserted his own "No Shit" in Pig Latin below it. Just the right touch. He wagged his head.

Randy knew it, felt it, could taste it, just as Berman could. Hard copy press and television is largely worthless. The day was coming when people would not read any newspapers, watch any television news, somehow they were becoming aware of at least this, there is nothing there for them.

The only reason anyone bought his paper was for the grocery ad, the local sports and the crime report. It would not be long now.

He would have to go back to teaching the truth of Nickostatos Greenberg ... or perhaps die.

He must fight on until.

"There is no time left!"

He jumped up as he remembered he was late.

CHAPTER TEN

"1492.

"As children we were taught to memorize this year with pride and joy as the year people began living full and imaginative lives on the continent of North America. Actually, people had been living full and imaginative lives on the continent of North America for hundreds of years before that. 1492 was simply the year sea pirates began to rob, cheat, and kill them."

— *Kurt Vonnegut*

"Who's going to New Town?"

"I am."

"Well, who's going with you?"

"Nobody."

"Take Harley with you."

"And hurry. There isn't much time."

Fulton Crampton exited the quiet, perfect, tile, marble and classical music Bouton Fiflin Starcourt ... Mace Yovonovich-Fofonovich Banana-fana Momonovich offices as he pushed the glass door onto the hard, cracked squawk of Broadway.

With tall, straight back and long, bleached white fingers barely gripping the thin briefcase at his knees he moseyed to the curb, waited for one-thousand-three for the yellow cab and got in.

At 30,000 feet Fulton Crampton eased his chair back, accepted his whiskey with cracked ice, put on his black eye mask patch, plugged in his earphones and remembered he had left Harland Lombardi.

* * *

In the meantime.

The eagle circled and drifted toward a distant ringing in the woods.

A ping, ping, ping like one solitary man building a railroad, trying to beat his best friend to Utah.

The old man mumbled, talking to the tree, apologizing as he pounded the spike with the sledge.

He talked again to the pines and oaks, maples, cedars and birch about the logging for the paper for the textbooks, sat down, looked up at a screech, pulled a handful of hard candies from his pocket, wiped sweat.

He heard the logging trucks roar.

He tossed two candies with bright red wrappers out a few feet.

"Come a little closer," he smiled as he growled.

He rolled over to his knees to be able to pull himself up by the tree, bringing his old backpack up with him as he stood. He ripped from the pack one of the torn hard covers of the sophomore history textbook, red, white and blue.

The old man set the cover on the backside of the tree, on the ground, where they wouldn't see it before it was too late.

In the meantime.

At The Times New Roman.

Nine of Nick's best historians clogged the back table, in the corner, in low light. The table was wood and thick and carved with sayings, epigrams, and epithets, and in the middle were pitchers and bottles and guacamole ... and chips.

They had heard what Nick was thinking, about holding up the release date on the new edition, perhaps ordering last-minute, last-second changes.

"If it's in The History Book, it's history!"

Phineus Jaggofff raised his mug and roared.

They cheered.

"Here, here!"

"You can't change that! Anymore'n you can change the weather!" stated Orimond Wicker, perhaps louder than he imagined.

"Marketing!"

"Sales!"

"Reconstruction!"

"We won't have it!"
"We'll go on strike!"
"Strike! Strike! Strike!"

The historians absorbed jaded glances from the next table where the Spine Gluers Union No. 374 was planning their own strike against 3B1K.

Of course, they would not want the damned lolly pants to steal their thunder.

But the historians in the big wood offices always talked about quitting or doing something that would shake the world, but they never did.

History is history. Same as physics is physics. Nothing to change. Just memorize it and move on down the hall to Typing and English 101.

The spine gluers of No. 374 pushed their stomachs farther into the table edge and clunked their heads together in their traditional toast.

Another roar went up from the back table as the history buffs had drifted into charades as always.

One fool perched on the table, squatting and depicting either the Lincoln Monument or Lewis or Clark in a canoe.

Completely overstating the case that the river or the canoe — or the paddle for that matter! — even existed at all.

As if it made any difference.

The spine gluers, the ones who held it all together, as the sign over their shop and on their grey work shirts said, had long, inherently, been engaged in discussions of existential philosophy.

Drifting out the doors of their little corner of the world, along with the smell of the glue, were thoughts and words, quotes, dreams.

"Does anything really exist though?"

"See, that's the thing."

"I know."

"Right?"

And they had finally targeted this edition.

The end of the world, everything.

There would be no American History 101, sophomore textbook, shipped from New Town all over America, because they would not stand for it.

"None of this shit is even real!"

They hissed and whispered as they glued the books together, taking deep breaths of the glue pots and the glue fires, the aroma and substance finding its way into their lungs, their coffee, their food.

They had put up with it, for years it seemed.

Nothing exists.

Somebody's making all this shit up!

I know, right?

And now it's going to all come a tumbling down on top'a their 'eads.

They nodded as one, clinked their glasses, clunked noggins and stood around the table, singing in hearty tones the Spine Gluers No. 374 union song.

Three of the historians stayed late, surrounded by chairs upside down atop tables. The bar man tossed them the keys, grabbed his coat and headed out.

The three made a walk-around, checking in the restrooms, under tables, behind the bar.

"History is heroes and wars and whatever the government does," one of them hissed freely.

"I know!"

"Race. Gender. Social Class. A narrative. It's rubbish!" hissed the second.

"You tell geography with a nice story? Here is where shit is, that's it!"

"The dumb fooking kids don't know their history and that's our fault? They want to only watch TV and wonder who's their daddy?"

"Our fault?" the other two chimed away impeccably on time like Big Ben.

"That's where it's all 'eaded."

"It can't be stopped."

"Unless."

One of them went to the bar, found three clean gigantic glass mugs, filled them and skillfully and not without a drop of Irish luck brought them to the table.

"Like what Rita said, at the meeting," one of them said to the others.

"If we could 'discover' (he made air quotes) a big mistake in the book, then that gets big publicity, and then we do a big thing about correcting it, then we get all this free notice of our history book, and all that better for us."

"Better yet," said another.

"We insert a gigantic gaffe, don't tell anyone, somebody finds it later and boom! the whole thing comes tumblin' down."

"Exactly," said the third.

"That is so right on."

"I know, right?"

CHAPTER ELEVEN

*"The finest workers in stone are not copper or steel tools,
but the gentle touches of air and water working at their
leisure with a liberal allowance of time."*
> — Henry David Thoreau

"Good morning! Daisy!"

Nick yanked open the glass front door, waved to his secretary, keeping far enough away that he could not hear what she said and she could not reach him with the notes and papers in her hands.

She got up, shot around desks, tables.

Usually Daisy forced herself to be perky as an Iowa dental office, but sometimes she just had to buckle down for both of them.

She stalked him between desks and file cabinets like a hummingbird that needed to eat.

He kept his heading, at times seeing her hair above cubicles, in a perfect line — standing on a chair, down again — to meet him at his office door.

Which she did.

She always did.

He paused, turned to Daisy, huffing, out of breath.

"Yes," he said.

She was also fatigued.

"You gotta ... go ... talk ... to Martha ... Mary," she said and handed him a neat stack of papers and notes and a single piece of paper with a single stick of Juicy Fruit.

He accepted the stack, dropped it where he stood and headed off with the gum and the single sheet.

Nick headed out the side door, to The Tower.

He walked over the lawn to the tall brick "I", which could have been a smokestack or a Middle Ages missile silo, but was not.

It was The Font Tower.

Nick trudged up the circular iron stairs, round and round.

The tower top was a wonder to behold, like a lighthouse, and if you were not right here right now you would not imagine the big clear window looking out over the river and the wood floor and wooden work tables and benches, where like monks with their letterpress Martha and Mary had toiled for decades. Some said the window came and went with the spirit of the viewer, but he could see it. The clouds looked funny because of the angle of the glass.

Their specialty, their love, their craft, was The Guttenberg Font, Old English? impossible to read, beautiful to look at. The ink smell here was different than other places in the plant, more predominant, organic here, embedded, like someone had bled ink into the brick and stone.

Maybe scented spit.

"Hello."

There they sat, as they had for centuries perhaps.

At a giant oak table, hunched over their work with their chisels, wood boxes of wooden letters, composing stick, mallet, and neatly stacked on the wooden benches around the room: hot metal, old church bulletins, wedding invitations, greeting cards, poetry books.

Nick clutched in his hand the one paper Daisy had given him that he had kept.

The notice that the last customer of Martha and Mary had died.

He walked to the old press, that required two people to operate, one to work the press, the other to ink the type. That is why Nick's grandfather had asked the two. That was his excuse, that he needed two people. Actually he thought they could protect each other by sitting back to back.

Well, you see, it was way back, back in the days of fast pitch softball and bowling leagues, when people talked to each other face to face, sat on front porch steps and talked to those walking by.

It was after World War II, the men were home, everyone was going to live long, great lives, have fun, play softball, go bowling, have happy children, paint the front fence white, all of that.

And Martha and Mary were the two best softball pitchers in town.

They were the leaders of the two rival women's athletic teams in town, The Chicklets and The Babey Ruths.

They waged low-intensive warfare over the summer on the hot diamond, and through the winter in the warm bowling alleys.

That lasted for a good long while, but then things started to change, not so you'd notice and then all at once, and the biggest sign of the change was slow pitch softball and grammar.

The plant had maintained an entire grammar department for many years, decades, and then gradually, and then all of a sudden, it got phased out.

It happened largely over "which" and "that."

A great controversy inside the walls of the plant that spread to the town and threatened to burn it down.

People arguing about which or that.

Martha and Mary, both being lively, educated young women, knew that which was sometimes better used over that, such as, you use "that" before a restrictive clause and "which" before everything else.

Some argued that is was more than that, more complex.

The battle raged and finally Martha and Mary were the only ones on the side of reason.

They were hunted down, stalked, stared at.

People burned "WHICH" in their front lawns.

People wore white T-shirts with THAT in big black bold letters.

Martha and Mary fought this battle at the same time as they battled each other on the diamond and in the alleys.

They kept at it for as long as they could, the softball and bowling, long after the "which-that" war was forgotten, into the Carter administration even, until The Chicklets and The Babey Ruths were the only teams left in town.

The bowling leagues faded out as well, so gradually that you really didn't notice, but one day they were just not there, leaving Mary and Martha, standing on opposite sides of the ball return. Some say Mary made the first move, some Martha, but they ended up drying their hands from the same alley and have ever since.

In the meantime.

The Moose Lodge opened itself to the public and served walleye every Friday for $5 all you can eat, just to keep the doors open. Nobody joined the clubs anymore. Neighbors did not go for walks to talk to other neighbors sitting on front porches. They locked their doors and huddled close to the television.

And for a while they, Martha and Mary, barnstormed the country, playing games against American Legion high school players using just themselves and a catcher.

When Nick's grandfather found them they were sitting on the third baseline bench at the old softball stadium.

Just sitting.

His tee shot from the ninth had drifted, again.

He walked up to them remembering how they were always together and there was one of them who was a bit famous in town for being able to calculate pretty accurately how much any amount of rain would equal in snow inches, and asked if they would come work for him.

Grandpa Greenberg had always wanted to use The Tower for something other than to store the old chairs confiscated from the middle school for the district not being able to pay its textbook bill.

And so he set Martha and Mary up as typesetters of the very old style, a side job, job printing, they called it.

They turned out perfect, as if it were what they were meant to do.

Their hands were strong as iron from bowling and pitching. And, well, with the things they could make a softball and bowling ball do, magical things, people called them both The Whiches of the Woods.

Maybe they would be able to use their mystical, monk like magic to watch over the company and the town from up there in The Tower.

It might be a stretch, but it was worth a try.

Which was the sentence that used to be on the company license plates and paychecks until everyone forgot what it meant and pressure was brought to bear on Nick to change it.

Actually, come to think about it, they did not start in The Tower.

They started out in papermaking and Nick's grandfather had no grand thoughts about their hiring, only needing warm bodies, so prob'ly maybe nobody really knows where all that other came from.

It was Nick's father who asked them to move to The Tower, that's right.

At least that's the story.

Parts of it, anyway.

Martha and Mary sat in the perfect light of the slanted window, still bent over working, wearing the Detroit Tiger caps, Martha's on straight over her shoulder-length white mane, Mary's on backward.

The Tiger cap had been their baby, their big project, years ago. It was their big ticket item until it got farmed out to a sub by some salesman who was no longer there anymore.

And now Mr. Droood had died.

The last customer.

Mr. Droood had ordered his funeral "cowboy cards" from Martha and Mary for a long, long time.

Nick nodded to them.

They showed their respect by holding their spit, not using the coffee can on the floor, between their feet.

He went to the window and leaned way back as one was wont to do in the presence of the angled glass.

Nick strained his back and began to hurt down by his waist, his lower back. He thought about coming back another day.

The M's were tough and it wouldn't get any easier, so ...

He had to close down The Tower.

We won't eat. We won't drink. We'll shit on the floor. Piss.

That is what he expected them to say.

"Nicky, come sit down."

"What?"

He straightened, really feeling it in the lower regions.

He walked over to them.

"Sit," said Martha or perhaps Mary. He didn't see any lips move.

Nick looked around for a chair.

He sat on the floor, not being able to see them way up on the other side of the table, but he saw their red high top tennis shoes and their Folgers spitoon.

There was no uniform at 3B 1K, but everyone was supposed to wear red tennis shoes of some kind – supposed to make work fun, and that was the common thinking of the Depression Era, when times were tough, that if the lights went out or there was a tornado or flood or someone had starved to death, or you had to pull someone out of a burning building, well, at least you could find them. That's the least we could do. And having the money to buy the more expensive colored shoes was a sign of prosperity, like a shined car in the driveway.

"We know about old man Droood."

One of them said.

Oh, boy, he thought.

He watched long lines of spit ...

They both began to talk excitedly.

"We've been anticipating this day," said one.

"As you might imagine."

"Yes," he said, pinching his butt to sit up higher, straining his neck, looking around for another chair.

"What about POD?"

They said together and giggled.

Nick leaned back on his hands and crossed his legs out straight.

He listened to them talk about print on demand, self publishing, desktop publishing, blogging, social media marketing tools.

"We would like to be in one of your more modern buildings."

"With the vending machines."

"On the ground."

"And a view of the golf course."

"The ninth tee is nice," said Nick.

"Yes."

"That's what we've heard."

Nick began to think that he could use some leverage and this might be just the ticket.

He stood and placed his hands on their table, to stretch and twist his back and neck.

"Would you mind doing something a little dangerous?"

"They looked at each other and back at him and smiled big together.

"Putting up a fuss about this for a while – and then bending to my will? It might get a little sticky."

"We'd love to bend to your will, Neeckolaaas."

"Danger is duty."

He told them his plan and they began to practice their lines.

I would rather die.

We won't eat. We won't drink. We'll shit on the floor. Piss.

Then we will die.

With justice and dignity.

Be it ever thus to tyrants.

CHAPTER TWELVE

"Fiction reveals truth that reality obscures."
— *Jessamyn West*

The red pickup turned into BBBK Drive, hitting the curb with one tire, tossing around the inhabitants, four large women stuffed like bread loaves into the front and Fulton Crampton in the back, sitting straight, his briefcase in his lap, his legs dangling out the back.

Fulton Crampton climbed down, waved to the women with their hands out the windows and stopped to take a look around: the statue elbowing out the marquee with the old sub-title, The Tower, the mill, the glassed office buildings, golf course, the hint of the river, the long, green hedge.

That might be new, he thought as he did one deep knee bend.

Fulton Crampton tried to remember how long it had been since he'd been here. He usually made use of the telephonic system.

Maybe he had never been here.

He walked into the nearest building, marked "Main Office" in subtle white Times New Roman on the glass door.

Seeing no one at the desks or cubicles he sat in a chair with his back to the window, his briefcase in his lap.

At almost the same time Harland Lombardi settled into a middle seat preparing for takeoff. Actually, he squeezed. He was not a small man. He closed his eyes.

Fulton Crampton wondered how long it would take Nickostatos Greenberg to appear in his own office, or anyone in the history book publishing business, for that matter.

51

He checked his watch and imagined Harley Lombardi squeezing his fists and eyes and toes to get the plane into the air.

This was all part of the annual book release dance. Fulton Crampton would make his call to Nick saying it was time to sell, that he should retire.

"Go fishing," Fulton would say.

"Relax. You're not going to live forever.

"Unless you know something we don't know."

The same thing every year.

Every year Nick would hang up without talking.

But this year was different.

For what reason Fulton Crampton did not know, just that his boss had sent him in person, told him to take Harley Lombardi with him and come back with BBBK in hand, which would give The Big New York Company almost total control of the sophomore history textbook market, which would put Fulton Crampton's Tuesday Afternoon Manhattan Club in control of what Americans would think, understand and believe for years to come.

Not that the textbooks of Nickostatos Greenberg were radical or socialist or communist.

They had all the right sub-titles, covers, study guides, the common chapters.

But sources had given indications that Nickostatos Greenberg had been walking around town, listening and asking, and walking around his company, listening and asking.

And that was never a good idea.

Harland Lombardi accepted the peanuts and a diet Pepsi he had coming, setting an elbow in a man's nose to get them. He did not look as he passed Pennsylvania, Illinois, Indiana.

Fulton Crampton looked at his watch.

He consumed a deep breath, faced forward, straightened his back, and without looking, itched his ankle with the edge of his shiny black shoe.

He raised his head, his chin, as Daisy appeared at her receptionist desk on the other side of the room. He stood to see over cubicle tops.

She waved and smiled and trotted the other way, her hair bouncing, on alert like the tail of a doe.

Fulton Crampton sat.

He pulled the peanut pouch from his jacket pocket, tipped his head, poured the contents into his mouth, keeping his eyes open, darting, looking for Nick Green.

He folded the plastic pouch and placed it onto the metal ashtray next to him. He tried not to stare as the folded bag slowly uncurled as if alive.

He heard the muffler of the red pickup and the crack of the four heads on the cab roof as the tire hit the curb.

Harland quick grabbed a pencil stub from his pocket and the peanut bag to write the number below the magnetic sign on the doors that said Airport Shuttle in case he needed to use their excellent services again.

Fulton Crampton nodded as Harland Lombardi sat in the chair next to him, moved his own chair to avoid Harland's arms.

"You were s'posed to get me," said Harland.

Fulton Crampton looked at Harland.

CHAPTER THIRTEEN

"There are two ways to be fooled. One is to believe what isn't true; the other is to refuse to believe what is true."
— *Søren Kierkegaard*

Nick stood at the podium, on the stage, in the company auditorium, where Willie Nelson had just played the day before as part of the ongoing lunchtime awareness program put on by HR/PR: "Bean Time Is Culture Time."

The seats were not nearly full because it was early, but he did not want to wander near his own office with Fulton Crampton and Harland Lombardi on double secret stakeout.

"Hello, hello. Is this on?"

The department heads were still finding their seats.

Nick came from behind the podium.

"He's here!"

He heard someone exclaim.

Nick sat on the edge of the stage.

He began to talk.

"We can't hear you!"

He fell to his back, rolled over, got to his hands and knees and crawled up by the podium.

"We can't see you!"

Someone brought up a stool.

He stood on the stool.

"Can any of you motherschmuckers hear me now?"

He whispered to himself, but it went out quite clearly.

He tapped the microphone.

"Oh, yes."

"Perfectly."

"Better than last year."

"Yes, I believe so."

They stood and clapped, gave Nick a standing ovation.

Nick put his mouth right over the microphone like a heavy metal singer.

"Anyone who doesn't sit the schmuck down right now I'm going to come out personally and pound. I don't care if you are a woman or elderly or what the hell you are."

He said like a rock star, and it worked so that they could not really hear him, only just get the gist.

They smiled. Some clapped. Some nodded and waved hello to those around them as they sat.

Signs had been set up around him in a semi-circle on easels from the art department.

"Seek not to arouse parents."

That plaque had come from the sales offices building.

"Who controls the present controls the past."

"The history book must inspire children with patriotism, must be careful to tell the truth optimistically, must dwell on failure only for its value as a moral lesson."

"Texas requires that textbooks shall not contain material which serves to undermine authority."

"The history of the United States shall be taught as genuine history and shall not follow the revisionist or postmodernist viewpoints of relative truth."

"American history shall be viewed as factual, not as constructed."

"The memory of oppressed people is one thing that cannot be taken away, and for such people, with such memories, revolt is always an inch below the surface."

"Don't want a book with an axe to grind."

"So, whatawegonnadonow?"

He spread his arms wide as a famous preacher might have.

They did not understand him. They looked at each other, leaned forward in their seats.

They must give him the answer he wants, but as was with Stalin, there were so many ways to displease him that perhaps the best one could do was to shoot oneself.

Nick hopped down from the stool.

He walked around the stage, gesturing, shouting. He sat again on the stage with his feet dangling, talking softly, pleading.

The department heads: Michelle Jones, Editing; Lori Groome, Art; Walt Anderson, Printing; Kolya Zuyev, Wood Products; Amos Chadwick, Research & Writing; Buddy Fowler, Maintenance & Landscaping; Cade Ewart, Crowd Control/Security; Kathryn (Bambi) Cartwright, HR/PR, sat on the extreme very edge of their seats, following his every move, wanting to give the immediate perfect response.

Austin Bellincioni, lead accountant, sat on an aisle step, hunched over a yellow legal pad, occasionally punching at an adding machine he had brought from his office.

Assistant executive assistant Daisy Doorknor paced the hallways, keeping an eye on Fulton Crampton and Harland Lombardi, relaying up to the minute reports to Executive assistant Joan McCarthy, standing in the hall doorway, hands across her chest, watching Nick Green on stage.

Nick asked someone to bring up a copy of this year's book.

He sat on the front of the stage, paging through.

"I have not actually looked at one of these things for years."

He looked up and smiled, a tear on his cheek.

"That was my sophomore year," he said.

"S'posed to be my sophomore year.

"I dropped out.

"To work here."

He laid the book on the wood next to him.

"You know there's actually a backpack law?" he said.

Several of the department heads wagged their heads up, down, enough for Nick to be able to see them nodding.

"They can't be this big, not really. Hurts the kids' backs just to carry them.

"Is it worth it? What we put in there for the kids, is it worth it for them to break their backs?"

"Lies My Teacher Told Me," he said.

"That's a real book.

"Just get through it. That's what some teachers hope for. Anybody read Harry Potter? You want to just get through it or did you enjoy it?"

Nick talked about drama vs. melodrama, the eternally optimistic approach to history, and how old editions are usually the same as the new editions.

"The best thing we have to offer kids is the sub-title," he said.

"And they suck. You know they do. Big-time. They are stooo-pid."

Nick hopped to the floor.

He held up a hand and smiled.

"Hey, you know I love you guys. I appreciate the work you've done.

"Thank you so much for coming out today to listen to an old man.

"Go back to your comfort zones, put in some real book publishing work in your nice little offices, get me some new ideas, or every schmuckin' one-a you is fired.

"Have a nice schmuckin' day.

"If any one-a you's claps you are fired right schmucking now."

Nick walked out of the auditorium straight to the boiler room where The Generals waited.

Nick sat on the barstool at the counter facing The Generals on the old sofa and chairs.

For an hour and a half they talked about Martians and Da War a da Worlds.

CHAPTER FOURTEEN

"Wrong does not cease to be wrong because the majority share in it."

— *Leo Tolstoy, "A Confession"*

Nick pushed into the restroom in the main office building and was greeted by the radio playing two different stations in the invisible speakers.

He had asked Daisy to play sports talk and classical and in order to not be wrong she always played both, which made for a confusing mix of ear candy. Nick liked it. It kept out the riff-raff.

He went to the stall on the far end.

Daisy had supplied him with "The War of The Worlds" and "The Mouse That Roared" stuffed inside the paper holder.

The writing in the stall was his, gossip about various employees, his way to vent.

But, what's this?

Somebody else's handwriting on the stall.

"He's serviceable."

Just what he had overheard his father saying about him regarding whether he was suitable to run the company.

The nearest speaker was playing sports talk. Nick liked the diversion away from serious stuff, but today he wondered how those guys can be that interested, ya know, in that, when other things are goin' on.

He found the black marker and edged forward to write something.

"Hey."

The marker clattered and Nick's stool banged when he jumped.

He sat, silent. His hand frozen in the air. His leg raised, his mouth open.

Nick's heart pounded out the quarter-seconds.

He leaned to his own wall to try to see under the divider.

He saw black tennis shoes.

"What are you doing here?" Nick said.

"Same thing as you, at least I presume."

"How did you get in?"

"I'm grandfathered in. I can come here whenever I want. It's a perk."

"You got anything to read over there?"

"I think it's the same old thing," said Nick.

"Let me look.

"Yeah, "War of the Worlds, Mouse That Roared."

"Oh, those are good ones."

"What you got?" said Nick.

"The Russians Are Coming, The Russians Are Coming. I think it's a play."

"Yeah, could be," said Nick.

"Over here they got Philip K. Dick, Ray Bradbury, Howard Zinn. "The Secret Life of B's."

A third voice piped up in the next stall down.

"What the?" said Nick.

"Who are you!" said the second voice to the third voice.

"Nobody, really."

"Don't be shy," said Nick.

"It's more like self-deprecating," said the second voice.

"Well, just a minute," said the third voice.

"Boom!"

He flushed, the powerful kind, like at a nice hotel, taking away everything, gone, bad memories, bad decisions, anything bad, away in a split moment.

"I am Bobby Barkham," said the third voice.

"You might have heard of me. Now who are you?"

"That's Nick Green. I'm Kamil K.

"Bobby Barkham," said Nick.

"Yeah, I have heard of you. Weren't you like the general manager of our school book depository when my father was the president? I don't think you were here when I came on board. Where'd you go?"

"Away," said Bobby Barkham.

"Away, away."

"And now you're back," said Kamil.

"Now I'm back."

"Why?" said Nick.

Bobby Barkham's banyo again boomed boisterously. The whoosh and roar took a full ten seconds to happen and subside.

"Geezuz," said Kamil.

"Speaking of Martians attacking New Jersey," said Bobby Barkham after the flush.

He put up double air quotes with toilet paper in one fist.

"I see you're having troubles getting out your new edition."

Nick glared holes through two dividers with laser beam eyes.

"It's like the Martians, right?" said Bobby Barkham from two doors down.

"How so?" said Kamil K.

"Americans thought they were being attacked by Martians 'cuz some radio show they trusted said they were, that's all."

"Boom! Whoosh!"

Kamil flushed and they waited.

"It just don't take that much, just sayin'," said Bobby Barkham.

His door slammed. The water in the sink ran. Kamil and Nick heard steps on the tile and the outside door open and close.

"What's that all mean?" said Nick.

"Don't you get it?" said Kamil.

"Nah, I don't."

"That was a message," said Kamil.

"And not just any message. It came straight from the top."

"I am the top," said Nick.

"Not so much," said Kamil.

"Listen, now. I know you don't like to listen, my old friend, but you are in a situation."

"Awright, go'head," said Nick, leaning back, stretching his legs, crossing his hands on his stomach.

Kamil K. leaned over, to put his mouth right next to the stall divider wall, like a priest giving extra-credit confessional advice.

"Incongruencies, absurdities," he began.

"Hyprocrisy," he said with an underline.

"It's all lunacy. Not the moon. Crazy.

"Take 'dis.

"We believe, we know, we are all going to die, but we act like it ain't never gonna happen.

"We take football and baseball very seriously.

"Money. Green paper.

"Jobs, all 'dat. You act like it was your freeking dream as a kid to sell insurance or drive a truck packed with bottled water. But you do it. It's schmucking nuts, right?

"Just think about it. Use your noggin for something else than a place to store that shitty schmuckin' Yankees hat fer crissakes.

"We eat cows, but not dogs.

"Yeah! Think about iiiitt!

"Indians. Dead. Nagasaki. Dead. Us. Not Dead. Yet.

"Think about it Nickostatos. The wait of the world is on your shoulders, bud. The whole world is waiting, for you. I'm serious.

"Sit up. Don't slouch."

"Boom! Whoosh!"

The door slammed, water ran for a moment as Kamil made pretenses of washing his hands.

"Who controls the present controls the past, Neecky,"

And he was gone.

"Or something like that," Nick whispered to himself.

Nick didn't even hear the door.

Nick Green sat up, leaned forward to pick up the black marker and scooted up on the seat to write on the door.

"Gone Fishing."

He sighed.

CHAPTER FIFTEEN

"Half of writing history is hiding the truth."
— Joss Whedon

Fulton Crampton and Harland Lombardi stood together like grossly fraternal twins attached at the shoulder and elbow, as Nick Green approached them moving fast, like Jack Ruby trying to walk from Dealey Plaza to Parkland Hospital to the Texas Theater to the sheriff's office all in one afternoon.

He moved fast. Arms just a pumping. They heard his labored breathing.

Nick turbo-walked because he had no idea where he was going.

He had to go so many places, talk to so many people, come up with so many genius ideas that he had no idea where he was walking to.

In fact, he found it enjoyable to run right into these two schmuckin' idiots, these assholes, because it gave him something to focus on.

In fact, he had never met them.

Fulton Crampton always made his threats by phone, and this other guy must be the muscle.

Beautiful.

"Hey, guys, glad you're here."

Nick walked right up to them and leaned over the plastic plants and the big yellow dump truck to shake their hands with both of his.

"Folla me fellas."

Nick walked into his office, around the big desk, full of papers and books, squeezing under the moose.

He sat, leaving Crampton and Lombardi standing in the doorway.

"Naahh, come in, come in," Nick waved like a New York traffic cop in a Nebraska town.

They moved to stand in front of the desk, looking around for chairs.

"So, you gentlemen are here to sell me toilet paper. Well, I think we like the service we are already getting, tell me why I should switch to your product."

Nick got up to lean over his desk, checking papers, this and that, waiting for them to answer.

Harland Lombardi got a look.

Fulton Crampton's chest expanded like a pufferfish, and subsided.

"We are not ass wipe salesmen, you ...," said Fulton Crampton.

Harland Lombardi pulled sunglasses out of an inside pocket, put them on, and reached his other hand inside his jacket and kept it there.

"We happen to be representatives of Bouton Fiflin Starcourt ... Mace Yovonovich-Fofonovich Banana-fana Momonovich, Mr. Green."

"Oh, ya don't say?" said Nick, sitting down, planting his feet up on the desk and pushing his blue and white Yankees cap up on his forehead with the tip of his thumb.

Harland Lombardi searched again for chairs.

Fulton Crampton gripped his briefcase with both hands and glared at Nick.

"It is time to sell, Mr. Greenberg," said Fulton Crampton.

"We are prepared to make you a fair offer."

Nick slapped his feet to the floor, flinging himself full up to the desk at the stomach level.

"I'll tell ya what, fellas," he said.

"You give me a thousand rolls to start, full-ply, at a fair price, we'll see how they work out, come back to me next year, maybe I'll have something for you then."

Harland Lombardi took one step toward Nick, keeping his hand inside his jacket.

"You will live to regret this," said Fulton Crampton.

"And maybe not," said Nick, twirling around to cross his arms over his chest and look out his window.

In the sub-title bunker, in the closed glass office of Deanno the manager, three men sat with half their butts on Deanno's desk, leaning toward Deanno's computer, listening to the conversation from the microphone in the left nostril of the moose over Nick's head.

In the art department restroom Lori Groome sat in the middle stall, her hands pressed to her head, listening to the headphones, blocking out the sports talk and classical music in the speakers, trying to hear something out of the old, defective microphone in the right nostril of the moose over Nick's head.

In The Historian's Conclave-Retreat-Big Library-With-Quill-Pens-Study seven men and two women sat with quill pens under individual tree lamps in big padded maroon chairs surrounded by walls of books to the ceiling, listening to the speakers that usually played Vivaldi, to the conversation now taking place in the office of Nick Green, from the microphone in the right ear of the moose over Nick's head.

And in the offices of White Bear-de la Rosa Realty, Honey White Bear-de la Rosa sat in her office behind a closed door, her feet on her desk, sipping white wine, wearing sunglasses, a cigar smoking in a green glass ash tray, listening to the local radio station broadcasting a live feed from the microphone in the left ear of the moose over Nick's head.

CHAPTER SIXTEEN

"I do not know what I may appear to the world, but to myself I seem to have been only like a boy playing on the seashore, and diverting myself in now and then finding a smoother pebble or a prettier shell than ordinary, whilst the great ocean of truth lay all undiscovered before me."
— Isaac Newton

Daisy held the glass door for Fulton Crampton and Harland Lombardi. Crampton clutched the briefcase at his waist with both hands. Lombardi accepted the door hand-off from Daisy, keeping one hand inside his jacket. The air smelled like rain and woodsmoke.

She stepped out, ducking against the light pelting, pointing downtown and again giving the directions to the café.

"You can't miss it!" she said.

Daisy shook herself off inside, knelt to pick up around where Fulton Crampton and Harland Lombardi had been sitting, and hurried to Nick's office to catch him before he left again.

She grabbed the door to stop, seeing that he was not there.

His head peeked up over the desk.

"I hear a buzz," he said.

"Looking for a bug, you know, a magnetic thing, oh, well, that's crazy talk."

Daisy held up both hands, tipped her head and shrugged.

He turned his cap back to straight and slapped his hands on his desk to pull himself up.

"Anyway," he said.

"The reporter will be here soon," she said.

"And a photographer I think."

"What?"

"I told you."

"Tell me again, please."

"From *Publishing Right Now*. I told you. Anyway, I'm telling you now. They will be here soon. If you want to hide, I'll tell them something."

"Why would I hide?"

"I don't know.

"I just thought ...

"It's Langley Harmsworth," she leaned close to whisper.

Nick drew a large breath.

"It's about dying publishers," said Daisy.

"I'm sorry. She was insistent. She called herself. I didn't know how to refuse, maybe I should ..."

"No," said Nick.

"I haven't been feeling so spiffy, maybe I should ..."

"No! No!" said Daisy.

"Not you, like publishing houses, the book business, general things, I think. I don't think she means you."

"Did I hear that Langley Harmsworth is coming?"

Hess Bangor poked his head out his door, right next to Nick's office.

He wore a blue ball cap with "Yankees" in white letters across the front, just like Nick's, with a blue suit, white shirt, red tie. His red hair was crew cut. His hands were covered in red freckles. He kept them moving, touching his pants, his tie, his neck, his cap, as if giving signs from the third baseline or trying to not let you see the freckles.

Hess Bangor, the Bangor legacy, seemed to always be in his office, nowhere else, never coming or leaving.

His role in the company was to have an office right next to Nick Green's office.

Up and down, up and down, all day long, as sometimes Nick closed his door and Hess Bangor would need to tiptoe over and stealthily try the door and perhaps nudge it open a bit.

Meanwhile, Randy hustled and huffed and puffed along the sidewalk carrying two bundles wrapped in twine. He stopped into the pharmacy to place one stack in his rack, take out last week's unsold papers, go up to the counter to collect his $2.25.

He shoved into the outside door and hit Harland Lombardi in the shoulder. Harland turned slowly toward Randy, his hand inside his coat, lowering his head to see over the top of his sunglasses.

Randy tilted his head, watching them as he walked on with them, both headed that way.

"You guys are from New York!"

Randy smiled, pleased that he had placed them.

"You're trying to get ol' Nick Green to sell the business!

"Well, good for you! That old douchebag."

Randy reached out to shake Harland Lombardi's hand as Fulton Crampton kept walking, looking at the stores for something that said "The Café or Le Café."

Randy tried to cut in front of Harland to get close to Fulton Crampton to ask a question.

Harland Lombardi hurried up to block him, stepped back to block again.

They came to the café.

Randy held the door for them.

"This is my last drop-off."

He held the newspaper bundle in one hand, with the twisted twine turning his hand blotchy red and white.

"I've got time for coffee, though. How 'bout it?"

Fulton Crampton and Harland Lombardi stared inside the open door at the rows of tables, each with four persons clutching white coffee mugs, all staring at them, some pointing, all recognizing the two men from the New York publishing company who had come to town to buy out the only remaining industry in town.

Fulton Crampton shook his head.

"No," was all he said.

Randy hurried inside ahead of the flapping screen.

Fulton Crampton and Harland Lombardi walked slowly, down the wide sidewalk, sometimes drifting toward the street, sometimes toward the brick buildings. Harland ran a finger along a bed joint in the brick.

Randy set up his brand new papers with the front page color photograph of the dead person in the body bag and the two super-surprised EMTs.

He set the papers out just so on the counter, in five stacks, like a brand new book at the bookstore, with the big, bold banner headline:

"WHO DEAD GUY BODY BAG?"

CHAPTER SEVENTEEN

"Frustration and Love can't exist in the same place at the same time, so get real and start doing what you would rather be doing in life. Love your life. All of it. Even the heavy shit that happened to you when you were 8. All of it was and IS perfect."

— *Jason Mraz*

A small man wearing a light blue shirt with a black tie, tan pants, black shoes, trotted around and around, down, the stone stairs, toting a torch that cast light and shadow on the stone walls.

The Castle, which nestled the seventh green, with its stone arches and towers, battlements, gatehouse, drawbridge and moat, housed the history department of Beantree, Barkham, Bangor ... Kruszynianys, Inc.

It had been shipped from Dundee, Scotland on a boat. Ol' man Beantree, Barkham, Bangor and Kruszynianys all went along and each stayed in their own tower, looking out over the sea the whole way back.

The moat was the little stream that started on the other side of town, ran around the seventh and ninth holes and emptied into the river.

An emergency Phi Alpha Theta meeting was being held that evening. It was supposed to be The Historian of the Year Award Toast, but ...

The honorary extinguishing of the electric lights and the subsequent lighting of the torches had already taken place, except for the torches, and the small man was in a big-ass hurry.

He clattered over the stone floor and lit the first torch and the light was quickly passed down by anxious historians in the robes and caps of their various universities to the torches along The Long Table.

They drank instant mead from thick pint glasses that were frosted an hour ago under a giant replication on a projected screen on the front wall – the dead Blaze Thornpine, his head being unzipped from the black body bag by four hands wearing blue rubber gloves.

The thing was, that the standard media manipulation event was supposed to have been just like every other year: boring.

Depicting some scene from history where someone gets killed. The newspaper covers it and everyone knows that the new edition is coming out and that they should buy their tickets for the Sub-Title Banquet and The Pageant and get their buttons to wear to show they bought them and not get rocks thrown at them by the local children, the whole town tradition.

But somebody messed up.

Somehow Blaze Thornpine, specialist Roman empire, also in the early stages of a larger project exploring the relationship between ecology, state power, culture, and social order in the Roman empire, had been the person running from the home on Fourth Street decorated in the front to look like the Ford Theater and shot, for real, to death.

By whom?

Why?

How?

Someone said it was Sonny the janitor, but someone else said, no, that can't be right.

"I would also like to draw your attention!"

Max Karp, head of the department pro-tem, stood at the far end of the table, not unlike a midget Dumbledore, in his purple robes, grey ruffled hair under his green floppy cap and the pool cue he used as a cane whenever he came to these meetings because of the slippery damp bricks.

He pointed with the blue end toward the new sign on the wall that could not be seen very well at all in the low light.

In any case, it said: WHATEVER HISTORIANS SAY IS HISTORY IS HISTORY.

Dramatically with a flick of his hips he ran the pool cue across as if an air underline to point at the other wall, where hung a banner that had been there for some time:

"If it's in The History Book, then it's history"

Someone hustled over with a chair for Max Karp, as he was not overly tall and some were complaining that they could not see or hear what he was saying, only the very top of his floppy green cap.

He stood on the chair with his pool cue.

He adjusted the floppy hat that wanted to get away.

Behind him appeared a screen on which the evening's discussion points appeared.

— The construction and maintenance of public myth

— Conspiracy Theory — so dangerous we must outlaw it

— Teacher — journalist — watchdog on power — that's their job — that's all we have

— The only thing that can rescue society are real historians

— The consensus hallucination that passes for reality

These were just an overview, a summary, a review that they went over every year during the closed portion of the Historian of the Year Award Banquet.

It was true, that Blaze Thornpine had been selected as historian of the year, that he should rightly be in the shootout and the body bag and when the reporter showed up at the traditional opening of the ambulance that he would take the photo of the unveiling of the body bag and Blaze Thornpine's smiling face would be on the front page of the local weekly newspaper and all would be well, cycles repeated, tradition, safety, remembrance, the start of the book production celebration and new fiscal year.

But not this time.

This year was different.

Moms and children were crying, people locking their doors, police cars seen in the streets, actually moving about town.

Max Karp yawned, pushing the pool cue way up over his head, and called for break time.

While everyone peed, all but two of the torches were put out, as they were about to enter "The Really Closed Portion Of The Night's Meeting."

Everyone scooted their chairs closer together, battling the brick and stone floor edges, and on the overhead projector behind Max Karp they saw the notes of the recent after-hours meeting of the historians at the Times New-Roman.

"The foo-foo version of history"

"History is heroes and wars and whatever the government does," one of them hissed freely.

"I know!"

"Race. Gender. Social Class. A narrative. It's rubbish!" hissed the second.

"You tell geography with a nice story? Here is where shit is, that's it!"

"The dumb fooking kids don't know their history and that's our fault? They want to only watch TV and wonder who's their daddy?"

"Our fault?" the other two chimed away impeccably on time like Big Ben.

"That's where it's all headed."

"It can't be stopped."

"Unless."

"Like what Rita said, at the meeting," one of them said to the others.

"If we could 'discover' a big mistake in the book, then that gets big publicity, and then we do a big thing about correcting it, then we get all this free notice of our history book, and all that better for us."

"Better yet," said another.

"We insert a gigantic gaffe, don't tell anyone, somebody finds it later and boom! the whole thing comes tumblin' down."

"Soooo," Max said, as he stepped down from the chair and put both hands on the table, looking around the table.

"I guess the idea is that if they are goin' to make all these changes, we are not going to allow it.

"It's history when we say it's history.

"Am I right?

"I said, am I right!"

He raised his pool cue over his head with both hands as the historians shoved their chairs back more violently than ever before, stood and shoved their thick glass mugs high into the air, right up the asses of the ones who would edit their copy.

"Aaaaah!"

Like hell they would.

The room grew quiet.

One of the two remaining torches flickered and died.

But.

Wait, just one darned minute.

There.

They all made eye contact with each other at once, glints of eyes passing back and forth across the table in the near-dark like disco night at the bowling alley.

Who put live ammo in the gun that shot Blaze Thornpine?

Who was the shooter?

He was supposed to be depicting how the traitor, the lone-nut traitor, murdered the president.

That could have been any of us.

Blaze Thornpine wasn't even interested in Civil War studies. He was an expert in the Roman Empire, and stuff like that.

Oh.

My.

God.

The last torch went out, perhaps from a breeze in an open high window.

Some say all the historians ran from the room, bumping over the torches, some with embers still burning hot, and that's what burned down the castle.

Some say it was lightning that struck the castle just as the historians were plotting to put in a subtle error in the history book on purpose.

Or which craft.

Some say we will never know.

Some few dare say, "Well, then, is this the year for our Cubs, huh?"

CHAPTER EIGHTEEN

"Human history becomes more and more a race between education and catastrophe."

— *H.G. Wells,* The Outline of History

The red pickup shuttle squeaked to a stop at the main building front door.

Langley Harmsworth pushed open the passenger's side door. Her photographer began gathering his equipment and saying goodbye and high-fiving the three large woman sitting with him in the hay.

Langley Harmsworth wore new stylish jeans with red cowboy boots and a bright red T-shirt with the *Publishing Right Now* name and logo. The shirt came to the top of her belly button and showed a hint of her Loch Ness Monster tattoo. Her hair was in a perfect blonde plait to the middle of her back, her eyes blue and on alert for metaphors, looking everywhere at once. She carried a black bag with her writing materials. Long red fingernails.

She stopped on the walk to look all around, and then headed inside, following by her photographer.

Langley Harmsworth did not smile when she introduced herself to Daisy.

"He's not in right now," said Daisy.

"Oh. I see," said Langley Harmsworth.

"Just when do you expect him to return?"

Daisy began to speak when a riding lawn mower roared past Nick's office window.

They turned back to look.

"Oh!" said Daisy.

"There he is! There he goes!"

She pointed with a long red nail.

Langley Harmsworth hurried outside, her photographer clattering in tow.

She stood on the sidewalk waving, trying to get Nick's attention.

He saw her and maneuvered the mower over, getting as close as possible to the building edge on the way.

He looked at her tattoo, then her face, then he turned the key to shut down the mower.

She did not smile.

She flicked her pen, tapped her toe on the cement and licked her lips.

"I heard you were dying," said Nick.

"What's that? No." she said.

"No. I heard you were dying."

"No," he said.

"Okay, seeya."

He reached to turn the key.

"No!"

She placed five red daggers on his hand.

"We've come a long, long way," she said in a slow, low growl.

"I meant the publishing business, Mr. Green, not you, per se."

"No, we're fine, fine. We're going to be just fine. Maybe in New York. Not here. We're fine."

He again reached for the key and pumped the foot feet.

"We got a tip," she said.

"This could be your last year if some things don't change," she said.

"I guess I could take up jogging," he said.

"Yes, you could go jogging," she said, "but why?"

"Then, it's not about me," he said.

"You don't want me to go jogging?" he swung his legs around to sit sidesaddle to face her.

"I don't care. Go ahead. Yes, why not?" she said.

"Okay," he said.

"Maybe later."

He again reached for the key to start the mower.

"No. Yes. It is about you. In a way. Why are you mowing? Don't you have a grass guy?" she said.

"Well, I'm mowing because it needs it, hasn't been touched since last fall. And, my grass guy takes his fishing vacation every year at this time. I always do the first few cuts. No big deal. Not really."

"Well, someone did say you were not doing well," she said.

"And you have been a sort of figure ... icon might be too much of a word."

She searched the clouds for content.

"It just goes with our whole recent theme.

"And we thought it would be fitting to ..."

She looked all around at the sudden activity that had sprung up around them as they had been talking.

Mary stood on the prim lawn, ankle-deep because Nick had not gotten that far yet, guiding Martha backing up a dump truck to the tower.

A splotch of white goo splatted the sidewalk and splashed on Langley Harmsworth's red cowboy boots. She looked up and saw an eagle circling.

When she looked down, squinting from the sun, Hess Bangor was standing right in front of her, in his Yankees cap, moving his hands around.

She looked at him.

"You all wear red tennis shoes," she said.

He looked at her.

"I'm just listening," he said.

A loud car pulled up behind them.

"Spraying for mosquitoes?" said Nick to the driver.

Kamil K chugged slowly past.

"Those who control the past, control the present," he said loudly, over the sound of NPR on his radio.

"Or something like that," shouted Nick in sing-song as Kamil pulled away.

Langley Harmsworth sniffed her nose like a bunny.

She turned to see the smoldering castle.

She put her hand on her brow to peruse the square of fence in the middle of the lawn with barbed wire on top, the sign that said deadly force would be used on trespassers.

"Is there a missile site on your grounds?"

"I'm not sure, but that's the sub-title bunker," said Nick.

Langley Harmsworth looked again at the eagle poop on her boot. She put her knees together to squat. She reached into the grass and came up holding a bullet.

Nick held out his palm.

She dropped the bullet into Nick's hand.

"That's a .45," said Nick.

"Glock."

Hess Bangor leaned in with his hands clutched behind his back.

He nodded and leaned back.

"Must be Harley Lombardi's," said Nick to Hess.

Hess nodded.

"Who is Harley Lombardi?" said Langley Harmsworth.

"Oh, nobody," said Nick Green.

"Just the hit man who came with Fulton Crampton from New York. I think they're down at the café having coffee."

Daisy ran up, stopped quick, handed the new edition of *The Journal-Times* to Nick and ran away.

"I thought I asked you to never ..." said Nick.

But she was gone.

He spread out the tab paper.

"Well, my gosh," he said.

"What?" said Langley Harmsworth as she moved around to read over Nick's shoulder.

She saw the headline and the full-color photo of Blaze Thornpine, wide-mouthed. One eye showing just the hint of being open, perhaps.

"Who is that!" said Langley Harmsworth.

"Oh," said Nick.

"That's one of our staff. Blaze Thornpine, The Historian of the Year."

Nick made air quotes while holding the paper.

Langley Harmsworth motioned to her photographer and gave him instructions to find lodging for them.

"We're staying," she said.

CHAPTER NINETEEN

"We have come out of the time when obedience, the acceptance of discipline, intelligent courage and resolution were most important, into that more difficult time when it is a person's duty to understand the world rather than simply fight for it."

— *Ernest Hemingway*

"I don't know much about history, and I wouldn't give a nickel for all the history in the world. It means nothing to me. History is more or less bunk. It's tradition. We don't want tradition. We want to live in the present and the only history that is worth a tinker's damn is the history we make today."

Fulton Crampton and Harland Lombardi sat on a bench on the knoll overlooking the park and the river.

"That's pretty good," said Harland Lombardi.

"I didn't know you knew that."

"That's not me. That's Ford. And it's true."

They stared together out at the river and the bridge, the thin highway.

"If it were me," said Fulton Crampton, "I would buy it and burn it."

"The river?"

"No, you, you ..., poor man, the company, the history book publishing company. And that's precisely why we are here."

Harland Lombardi pulled his hand from inside his jacket to pound his pockets.

"You do not need matches, sir," said Fulton Crampton.

"We have a torch."

Fulton Crampton stood for a moment, pulled out a money clip from his inside jacket pocket and sat down again.

He removed the clip from the roll and twisted the money into a cone.

He pulled from his outside jacket pocket a red lighter.

Eager-beaver seagulls dashed past. A truck blew its horn. The smell of the bakery caught their attention for a moment, and then not so much as fire.

He flicked it and tilted the money twist cone into the flame.

Fulton Crampton held up the flaming money torch like a seated Libertas.

"Hey!" said Harland Lombardi.

"Hey! That's money!"

He stood and jumped all around the flame, wanting to do something.

The fire reached Fulton Crampton's fingers.

He dropped the burning pile to the ground.

Fulton Crampton stomped it.

"Money," said Harland Lombardi.

"That is money."

Fulton Crampton and Harland Lombardi sat watching a man and his son in a rowboat on the river, fishing poles dangling into the water.

The smell of cash, not unlike burnt batter or old tomato soup, swirled between them at their feet.

Fulton Crampton and Harland Lombardi sat like men at a campsite, not needing to talk, just watch the fire.

Fulton Crampton sighed, enjoying the moment, and then squinted against the smoke in his eyes when he found that Harland Lombardi needed to talk.

Harland Lombardi, who had lots of time on his hands nearly every day back at the office, waiting, had taken to studying as of late, perhaps unknown to Fulton Crampton, perhaps not.

He talked about Daniel Boorstin and his books, Doris Kearns Goodwin, Ken Burns, Tom Hanks, about their history books and their television shows and their cookbooks.

Harland Lombardi had never had such a good listener as Fulton Crampton, who watched his money fire fizzle and stared out at the moving water, and the father and son, who had anchored toward the shore, out of the current.

"It's really interesting," said Harland Lombardi in apparent conclusion.

Fulton Crampton opened his mouth to add or rebut, but Harland Lombardi plowed on.

He talked about New York, about bigness, and about this small town they found themselves in today, and about smallness, and then about personal feelings of bigness and smallness.

"Macro."

Fulton Crampton moved his lips.

"Micro."

"Why do you want to kill history?"

Harland Lombardi turned toward Fulton Crampton.

Harland Lombardi noticed that Fulton Crampton noticed that his hand was not inside his jacket. He made the correction.

Fulton Crampton chewed his teeth and deigned to turn toward Harland Lombardi, keeping his knees together, the briefcase in his lap.

"I don't want to kill history," he said.

"It's business."

Fulton Crampton looked down to the water and saw that the man and the boy in the boat was now just the boy. Maybe the father had fallen in, maybe drowned.

It had begun to rain.

The boy turned to the rope and began to haul up the anchor.

It thundered and rained harder.

"Follow me," said Harland Lombardi.

He hunched and ran toward the downtown, following the smell of the bakery as he had learned in the Army, which isn't that easy.

The bell on the door rang as Fulton Crampton and Harland Lombardi pushed into the tiny tight shop, neat, overly decorated, smelling like cookies and bread ... pie, and frosting.

They stood in line looking straight ahead, at the small round woman with white hair smiling, waiting on the lucky first person, studying the brand new pastries in neat rows in the glass counter case.

"And, it's more that," continued Fulton Crampton, "as Henry Ford said, it doesn't matter. It's past. It's gone. What is happening is today, and then tomorrow. That's all there is. The rest is bunk."

Harland Lombardi shuffled up, then again as they reached the front of the line.

Fulton Crampton looked down as someone behind him was pressing too close.

He saw Hess Bangor, whom he knew from, somewhere.

"Wow, those look good!" said Harland Lombardi, pointing to the cookies on the front counter in the shapes of the heads of George Washington and Abraham Lincoln.

"Pre-History Cookies!" said the woman as she placed two into a bag and handed it to Harland Lombardi.

"It's that time of year again!"

Harland Lombardi turned with his bag and looked up at Fulton Crampton.

"I don't think I see it that way," he said.

CHAPTER TWENTY

"Today the world is the victim of propaganda because people are not intellectually competent. More than anything the United States needs effective citizens competent to do their own thinking."
— *William Mather Lewis*

"Nice shot, girly girl."

Martha marked an X for the strike as Mary strolled back with a big smile on her face.

They wore black and white "WHICH" T-shirts with blue jeans and tennis shoes.

Mary wore her long grey hair in a ponytail.

Cigarettes smoked in the ashtrays.

They clinked beer bottles, chugged the last. Mary jogged with the empties up to the bar and brought back more.

They talked while they took turns bowling and keeping score, high-fiving as they passed on the lane.

The backs of their black shirts showed a white witch's hat and below it in very small type, in Guttenburg font:

"... [dissidents, rebels, revolutionaries, idealists] ... we didn't start the fire, but we're burning."

"You know," said Mary as they sat together in the two chairs after their first game.

Martha figured the scores.

"That POD might work out. A lot of people think they are writers, could be lots of work."

"I'll miss the old type," said Martha.

"The window, the wood, the ink, the steel."

"The silence," said Mary and they clinked their bottles.

Martha took Mary's bottle and got up for the next round.

Mary saw that she had been sitting on the latest edition of *The Journal-Times* with the front page color photo of Blaze Thornpine's head in the body bag.

She flapped it open to read as Martha pushed up to take her shot.

CHAPTER TWENTY-ONE

"Facticity is a concept defined by Sartre in Being and Nothingness as the in-itself, of which humans are in the mode of not being. This can be more easily understood when considering it in relation to the temporal dimension of past: one's past is what one is, in the sense that it co-constitutes oneself. However, to say that one is only one's past would be to ignore a significant part of reality (the present and the future), while saying that one's past is only what one was, would entirely detach it from oneself now. A denial of one's own concrete past constitutes an inauthentic lifestyle, and the same goes for all other kinds of facticity (having a body—e.g. one that doesn't allow a person to run faster than the speed of sound—identity, values, etc.)."
— Sign on old, weathered bulletin board in the glue department, along with "All Employees Wash Your Hands" and "In Case Of Nuclear Attack, dive under work benches" (someone had penciled in: put yer 'ead 'tween yer legs 'n ...), "Don't Eat Snow!" "Stop, Drop & Roll," note, in old parchment, curled, partially burned from the glue fire of 1949

Forever the spine gluers had labored in The Dungeon, under the river, to keep the toxicity and smell of the glue pots, epoxy away from the general population of the publishing plant.

They wore long leather aprons, Steel Toad Boots, the best quality union footwear, from Vermont, long hair, and long fingernails. They all looked almost the same, on the short side, thick, with strong hands.

Passed down in families, these union jobs.

But it's time.

It's time.

"It's been time!" somebody shouted.

The Tuckins, Cozzees, Cotton, Brandybucks, Boffins, Fairbairns, Bolgers, Moons, Turns, Nouwens, Doorknors.

Belba, Bodo, Bungo, Celandine, Doderic, Dora, Tolman, Tobold, Pearl, Moscow, Turin, Tallahassee, May, Lily, Daisy and Harding.

The available names just repeated, generation after another.

In the meantime.

Now was The Time Of Waiting.

They tried to stay busy by some odd jobs, but they hated cleaning and too much moving about led to getting stuck, on a wall or a bench or the ceiling and what good were you to anyone then?

So, they found a dry spot and stayed put, smoking, philosophizing, napping, taking deep Zen breaths and pulling the fumes down, into their lungs and their blood and their brains and their toes.

When they went out at all, it was to two places, to the Times New-Roman or to Kwik Stop for orange pop.

Or to steal.

Then, three places.

They wore sunglasses, Oakleys, gotten-got from robbing from the rich who left their things inside their cars, and giving to themselves.

When going out for drink, they tied a tiny almost invisible thread that ran around each other and to each other and all the way back home. A tug on the thread meant it was time to come home.

Sure, but it was the glueing they lived for, that they were born for. It was the waiting that killed them. Many had died over the years.

And perhaps they had just about had it.

Or, someone had had a vision. A god had sat just above the river and told them that this shit had gone far enough.

Perhaps someone came up with this idea of revolt because it sounded better than quitting, going to the top and giving up on real life. There was honor in rebellion and also an end to waiting.

Or, maybe it was just an idea whose time had come, finally and for all.

They also lived in the tunnels under the river, not in town, not in the housing provided by the company for some of the workers along the fourteenth hole.

It would be right and good to say that they had their own finely-honed culture under the earth, a language and art and literature, with carts that rode giant rail lines and they had cute, blind ponies to ride, if they did, but they didn't.

They sat and they glued.

And they pulled down.

Gardens from above, fish from the river, and justified it in their own minds by saying they had no light and no sun to grow their own.

And that was good enough to satisfy their own minds, which is all that actually mattered.

And so, they came to work and waited.

That is what they did, all day long, until finally the collated pages would come sliding down the chutes, around and around, flying down and they would work all day and all night, much like Santa Claus or The Easter Bunny, perhaps, until the job was done and then, they would wait.

Nothing exists.

Nothing.

We must stop this façade, this fantasy.

This phantasm.

That's it, exactly.

With glue everywhere, despite all their moderate efforts to clean, sticking to everything, it was hard to get up and down, or walk.

All around, here and there, some were stuck to walls by their shoulders, on toilets. The sticking was a moderate danger, and rather than fire extinguishers they had spatulas, from regular-sized to giant, two-man.

And so, now, what are we going to do.

We know we must do something.

We won't glue.

It's eating away at us. We can't take it anymore!

Anything.

Nothing.

We are important.

Everything will fall apart.

As it should.

As it must.

Sic semper el mundo.

CHAPTER TWENTY-TWO

"Your time is limited, so don't waste it living someone else's life. Don't be trapped by dogma — which is living with the results of other people's thinking. Don't let the noise of others' opinions drown out your own inner voice. And most important, have the courage to follow your heart and intuition."

— Steve Jobs

They were almost there.

Almost all there, in the car.

The company 1958 black and maroon Pontiac Bonneville convertible.

The top was down and they were just waiting on Antoinette.

And Chuck.

It was that time of the year again, when Stan would walk over to the garage and get out the company vehicle, the last remaining, that old man K. had bought for the company.

It was there, somewhere, in the company's bylaws that the sales staff drive to the local school board book purchase meeting in the car. Other meetings in other towns and states could be gotten to however.

It was supposed to give credibility to the staff, display pomp and status, but these days who knows what it displayed.

The seats and back cushions were very cushy, and nice.

Stan ran his palms lovingly all around the giant white steering wheel.

Jean hunched low in the front passenger side.

Cid waited on her cousin Antoinette, kneeling in the backseat, looking everywhere.

Jean muttered, "Hey, Stan."

Stan said "what" and looked, just as Chuck jumped over the side, kicking Stan in the face, as he did about every other year.

Stan wiped mud from his forehead as Jean ducked and searched for a radio station from the '50s on the dash.

"There she is!"

Cid pointed then waved as if Antoinette were the last survivor from a burning building.

Antoinette wore a scarf around her hairdo.

She climbed in the backseat.

And away they went, at five mph around the horseshoe drive.

"We're just going to the school. We should walk," said Antoinette.

"It's more healthy, just contributing to the ozone."

They passed the sub-title bunker and saw Deanno mowing the lawn. He stopped and stared when he saw the Bonneville moving, perhaps knowing that the time was drawing yet more nigh, when he would need to order those triangle sandwiches for the sub-title banquet.

They passed Fulton Crampton and Harland Lombardi walking back, looking sweaty. Fulton Crampton gestured as he talked, and Harland Lombardi looked at Deanno on the stopped mower.

Honey White Bear-de la Rosa paused in front of her office and stared, rubbing with one hand what looked like a white poodle around her bare shoulders.

Kamil K. sat low in his faded green Pontiac on a side street, watching the sales staff head to the meeting, thinking, wondering, almost nodding off.

Chuck turned up the hill toward the school for The Special Spring Morning Meeting With The Board.

"So. What's our plan?" Chuck said as he pulled to a halt on the curb in front of the big brick building.

"What do we have that's new?" said Cid.

"What's our big pitch?" said Antoinette as Jean fussed with the radio.

They sat in the car, not watching the building, studying the four-way, cars stopping, waiting, going.

They waited.

Jean flicked off the radio and sat back in a huff and wrapped her arms under her bosom.

Antoinette unwrapped her hair.

Cid checked her nails.

Stan touched his tie and his hair.

Chuck ran his pointer finger all around the wheel without losing touch, even on the way down low.

"Okay," he said.

"I think we're ready."

They took some time climbing out of the two-door, negotiating the muddy terrace, and marched in, leaning forward, not walking together, yards apart.

Their shoes echoed in the long, wide, shiny hall.

At the end of the hall, through the big windows they could see the school board waiting, watching them, every step.

The 3B 1K sales staff sat at a long table in front of the board's long and wide table.

"We have no money," one board member began the meeting.

"Don't need any more books," said another.

"Got plenty," a third board member completed the rehearsed opening statement.

"Yes, but B3 1K is a pillar of the community!" said Cid.

They went back and forth with that theme for ninety-two minutes, the board saying they did not need more sophomore history books, that the new ones were always the same as the old ones anyway, that they would consider putting in another order when the covers for these fell off, and they need new volleyball jerseys.

Principal Miss Bordeaux, sitting alone in the back, smiled to herself, then resumed her stark countenance before anyone saw.

"Thank you very much for coming in," the board president said.

The sales staff took turns crying and staring hard and not quite pounding their fists.

At lunch time Antoinette, Chuck, Cid, Stan and Jean sat again, in different positions, in the black and maroon 1958 Pontiac Bonneville company car, on the curb in front of the old, giant brick school building.

They watched the traffic waltz and dipsy-do around the stupid schmucking four-way.

They decided against going out for lunch.

They decided not to go out Friday for drinks. They decided to go out now.

They decided not to tell Nick Green.

Antoinette dropped them at the front door of the main building to get their shit and smoked the tires taking the Bonneville back to the shed.

CHAPTER TWENTY-THREE

"It was only in the 1980s when I began to do serious research that resulted in my first book, which later became Killing Hope, that I was able to fill in the details and realize that the United States had indeed masterminded that particular coup or assassination, and many other coups and assassinations, not to mention countless bombings, chemical and biological warfare, perversion of elections, drug dealings, kidnappings, and much more that had not appeared in the American mainstream media or school books."

— William Blum

"So, when is The Big Sub-Title Banquet Shindig?"

Lori Groome completed a tricky air-quotes-while-holding-plastic spoon-and-fork maneuver.

Deanno put his finger into the air to say that he needed just a moment.

He sat with Groome, the cover art department manager, in the cafeteria, with the plastic knife, the only one for the whole table, it seemed.

"'S'posed to be soon," he said.

"Not sure of the date, soon.

"What's the title?"

"Duh, it's always American History 101," she said. "Year-in, year-out."

"Yeah, you're right, duuhhh."

They chewed, bent over, at the metal tables, like moderately evolved

Holsteins.

"Why doesn't the front cover get something?" he said.

"A banquet or, something, I wonder."

"I wouldn't want it," she said.

"What a bunch of ..."

"Yeah, I know, right?" he said.

"You do have the cover art show, though."

"That's nothing," she said.

"It's just putting up the same frames on four walls in the Bangor Memorial Room, nobody comes. Why would they?"

"Yeah, I know," he said while knifing peas onto a spoon.

"I do have to order some-a those schmucking his'try cakes, that reminds me," she said as she shut herself off with a fork of broccoli.

They watched each other's back while scooping, piercing, chewing, swallowing, then big breath, look around, head down again.

"I was going to try something new," she said, pointing at Deanno's nose with a doomed red grape on her fork.

"Ya know, but now! Shit."

"Whatdya mean, L.G.?" said Deanno, wiping his chin with a napkin and waving at someone.

She looked, partially, not enough to see who he was waving to.

"We have all we need, all we ever need, right here."

"Yeah-huh?"

"But if what I've heard he's planning is true, I don't know how we're going to do that. It's not going to work. We're goddamned-schmucked!"

She pushed her stomach into the table and hissed, not looking around to see who was noticing.

Deanno waved with both hands high and smiled, then looked at Lori Groome.

"Schmucked what? Have you heard what the sub-title is going to be?"

"No! Of course not!

"Nobody has! It's all schmucked-up. It's schmucked! It's schmucked!"

"I know, right?" he said, trying to give attention to Lori Groome as well as the members of the sales team who were dragging in.

He motioned for them to come over.

"Come on! Come on!"

Stan kept up his lonely sojourn toward the salad bar.

Chuck and Cid excused themselves, cut in front of people, making their way toward Deanno and Lori.

"So," said Deanno when they got within hissing distance.

"How ... did ... it go?

"Huh?"

Cid and Chuck sat together on Lori's bench.

They put their hands on the table and looked around.

"That good, huh?" said Lori, smiling, shaking her head at her lettuce.

"Oh, shit," said Cid, looking over Deanno's shoulder, then ducking.

They turned to see Nick Green prancing into the cafeteria with Langley Harmsworth, her photographer, Fulton Crampton, and Harland Lombardi.

Nick smiled and pointed at them.

"I better pee," said Chuck as he got up.

"Weren't we goin' T-R anyway? Let's just go."

"You can't lea ...," Cid reached for his jacket and missed.

"Well, looks like we're all here!"

Nick pranced over, trailing his entourage, throwing his arms, puffing out his chest like the new little guy on the cellblock trying to not be killed yet.

Deanno, Lori and Cid sat in silence.

Cid looked over her shoulder for Chuck or Stan.

"So!" Nick said.

"I'm ordering triangle sandwiches and folded napkins. What else do I need?"

"Um, for what?" Lori turned to look at him, chewing lettuce.

Nick picked something from her lip.

"Well, the big banquet, that's what!

"Right, Deanno?"

"Yep, right," said Deanno.

"Can't wait."

"Well, there is no time for waiting," said Nick.

"Rest is for the wicked," he said.

"I know, right?" said Cid, trying her best to smile.

Nick stood with his hands on his hips, a big smile on his face, trying to think of what the schmuck to do now, how to handle Langley Harmsworth, her photographer who was now under the table snapping photos of everyone from creative angles, Fulton Crampton and Harland Lombardi.

And he had not heard a word about how the sales team meeting went and from the looks of Cid he didn't want to ask.

They all turned at the sound of clattering shoes on the shiny tile.

Like Dorothy out of breath, stumbling to the finish line of The Yellow Brick Road Marathon came Daisy with the ubiquitous piece of paper in her hand.

"It's schmucking Pheidippides," muttered Fulton Crampton as Daisy held the paper up to Nick and grabbed her knees.

Nick took the paper and thought about crushing it, but rather held it inside his fist while searching the cafeteria for a way out and asking Langley Harmsworth how her room was at The Super Five.

"It's The Spine Gluers," Daisy gasped out a breath.

"Oh my schmucking Christ," Nick said to himself, looking at the far wall where a mural of the entire plant had been drawn by Lori Groome four, five years ago.

"Union ... Number ...," said Daisy.

"Three! Seventy! Four!" said Nick as he swirled around to face everyone again, threw up his arms and held them out as if herding motherschmucking sheep.

"Well, let's continue on, then," he said.

"Let's keep 'er moving, shall we then, huh?"

Like a teenage party just after the adults have left, the cafeteria buzzed.

And shut down just as quickly as there, in the doorway, blocking any exit, especially an exit by Nickostatos Greenberg, stood The John Brown.

CHAPTER TWENTY-FOUR

"When you control the means of information and effectively the investigation, the coverup is easily ... and the media as well by the way, does not get involved in investigative journalism anymore of this sort ... you control the results, and you control history. You rewrite history. You write it for future generations, and that is where we are."

— *William Pepper*

John Brown's white cowboy hat brushed the doorway header as he entered the cafeteria.

He surveyed the room, a german shepherd under one arm and a Pantone color fan in the other.

He chuckled big and deep, rumbling like a glacier about to tumble.

The John Brown.

He exuded self-esteem, confidence and years of therapy, sales seminars, morning TV yoga programs, and back-country kayak weekends.

Like a real-life Paul Bunyan, he held the german shepherd and pantone wheel and smiled across the wide and deep cafeteria.

He still held the unofficial record for the high school for the longest lasting, smelliest fart.

And as far as Lori Groome was concerned, he'd let it go to his head. Upon seeing him again, she went back to poking at things on her green tray.

He wore red flannel shirt, blue jeans and boots.

He was rarely seen in these parts, most often on the road in his capacity of Head of The Margins & Spacing, Paper Thickness & Color, Focus Group Consortium.

On the front of his cowboy hat a sticker read: "Vietnam Veteran: If You Don't Know Your History You're Destined To Repeat It." *Wall Drug.*

Lori Groome and others from his high school class called him "chameleon," realizing he always reflected the views and opinions and garb of the last person or group he had talked to. Sometimes he had appeared back in town dressed as an Hawaiian Native, an Iowa farmer, Native American, urban youth.

Nick had seen him maybe two, three, four years ago. He had an office somewhere, some kind of staff, was gone lots of the time. Which was fine.

"Roaaarrr!"

He bellered like one of those guys on the TV program trying to find Bigfoot, or a giant finding tiny people in his cloud castle.

Randy the reporter sat off to the side, taking a break in his kitchen worker disguise. His mop and bucket sat nearby, his paper hat and fake nose-sunglasses on the table as he gulped down his sandwich in lurches like a dog.

John Brown had stepped atop one of the metal lunch tables.

He spread his arms wide.

Lori Groome could not help herself. She turned around to watch, wondering where has he been?

Holding the german shepherd under the one arm, he raised the Pantone color fan high in the air with his other hand.

"The Secret Book of Presidents!" he roared.

Randy looked up, his mouth wide and full of bread and lettuce.

"Notes! Written inside a history book!

"Who wrote them!"

"I dunno," said Lori Groome to herself.

"History is so boring!" cried John Brown.

"Who could say that!"

"Well," said Lori Groome to nobody but herself.

John Brown stalked back and forth on the table and certain people began to worry about him going too far and the other end of the table catapulting or flipping into the buffet lineup.

He talked more about the handwritten notes found inside of one of last year's sophomore history textbook: about teachers just going through the motions, trying to get to the end of the book before the end of the year, more about The Presidents Book of Secrets, Plato's Cave, things of that nature.

John Brown jumped.

He threw all he had toward the next table and hit the landing with just a minor deduction for slipping with his cowboy boots on the slick metal.

He stood over the historians, all dressed today for some reason as their favorite character in history.

"You!" said The John Brown.

"Death! Destruction!

"Stalks you.

"Textbook gaffes indeed," he said so that just the historians could hear him.

"Boom! Boom-boom-boom!"

John Brown stomped the metal picnic table with his boots, one ... then the schmucking other one.

Daisy, standing within the Nick Green party, recognized that he was attempting to draw the attention of Union No. 374, as they would certainly have their ears glued to their ceiling to hear this.

She tapped her toe as hard as she dared, doing just what she could.

"Eckhart Tolle!" he boomed and Daisy thought that name sounded a bit familiar.

"Nothing has happened in the past; it happened in the Now. Nothing will ever happen in the future; it will happen in the Now."

With that The John Brown stepped down, put the german shepherd and the Pantone color fan on the floor and bench beside him.

Nick Green and his group made their way out of the cafeteria, and the very nonspecific happy buzz resumed.

John Brown set his fists on the table like two mugs of beer.

He waited, waited, looked around, then threw a leg up over the bench, stalked to the buffet line and took a tray.

CHAPTER TWENTY-FIVE

"Whoever controls the media, the images, controls the culture."

— *Allen Ginsburg*

K. Kruszynianys slumped in his Faded Green Pontiac at the A&W drive-in, slurping a Root Beer Float from a straw and a plastic cup.

Just his eyes showed above the window, watching pretty much everything.

He'd been cruising main all day long, watching, searching, seeing.

He heard chirping, like a flock of crows finding a piece of white paper.

He switched hands with the root beer and rolled his window up an inch.

Honey White Bear-de la Rose sashayed by with the other members of The Daughters of the Last Century.

As they passed on the sidewalk she sniffed the air and then spotted him.

Their eyes met.

He slumped farther as she turned and bounced along with her group all in their big yellow and orange dresses.

Hess Bangor perched at his desk like a parakeet with too much on its mind, not blinking, eating his jelly sandwich by pecks, holding it with both hands.

The system is not stupid, he thought as he chewed and stared into space. The reason for all the listening is that they are anticipating, trying to gauge the anger, anticipating, waiting, to see what is happening ... and trying to stay ahead of developments.

Next to his baggie of carrots sat his yellow legal pad and pencil, where he marked the movement of everyone, but especially Daisy because he saw her mostly.

She is the key.

Or not.

He scratched it out, then wrote it again, holding the sandwich for a moment with just the one hand.

He listened in the bud in his right ear to the happenings in the cafeteria, and in his left ear he heard the Spine Gluers having one hell of a time getting Bungo Cotton unstuck from the ceiling just underneath the cafeteria floor.

The boy pointed and the man saw the eagle.

The man continued rowing while the boy fitted a new worm onto his hook.

They did not notice the men teeing off on No. 9 who did not see either the eagle or the fishermen.

The eagle saw the fishermen and the golfers.

It circled slowly without moving its wings.

It smelled the book publishing company and felt the sun. It heard the turning of the keys and the starting of the engines.

The Beantree Barkham Bangor ... Kruszynianys delivery trucks pulled one at a time out of the garage.

The white trucks, all dripping from just being washed, sported the 3B 1K logo on both sides along with the image of the tried and true sophomore history textbook cover with the faces of Washington, Lincoln, Jefferson, the flag, the apple, and a teacher's desk and blackboard.

They lined up in front of the main building for The First Rehearsal when the books would come flying off the presses into the boxes, onto the pallets and forklifts and into the trucks, to would take the story of The United States of America straight to every big and small school across the country who could pay for it.

The back double doors of the trucks said How's My Driving? and told the story of the company in a tight little paragraph, and then:

"He who controls the present controls the past."

The old man in the woods saw the eagle and how she was looking down toward where the main building would be and he knew.

It was that time of year again.

Well. It just was.

One more little tap-tap, and he picked up his tools, his bag of spikes, and darted into the woods, invisible in a moment.

Pickup doors banged, in the way back a truck coming down the road, still far enough.

Talking, laughing.

This is where the ribbons were, where they would begin their day.

The saws whined and whirrrred and the cedar smell soothed the air.

He watched, Bigfoot style, branches masking his face.

A young man, working hard, ahead of the rest, pulling his trigger, getting ready, approached the bait trees, the kill zone.

He wore his yellow hardhat backwards. The name on tape said "Smitty."

He had a tattoo on the back of one hand. He was small and feisty, a good kid, the old man could see. The old man considered for a moment his own tattoo, on the inside of his forearm, The Statue Of Liberty.

The young kid took the saw in both hands, determined to do a good job.

The old man saw his whole life in front of him, the kid. How he had come through some tough times, fought back, got better, landed this nice paying job, wanted to make his life better.

And when he hit the spike in the cedar the blade would kick back right into his face, and before he could draw it away with shaking hands it would tear away his face, his nose, prob'ly his eyes, at least one for sure. Blood would be suddenly everywhere, the trees, the brush, the ground. The wound on the young man would be something the other workers could not imagine, could not believe though it was right there, on the ground, at their feet. There through the blood and the skin, see? his throat and his brain.

They would run everywhere just to be moving, just running, like ants in a time of tragedy, around and around.

And maybe the young man would die, on his back, his arms outstretched and maybe it would happen quickly.

It should.

If there is a God.

It would.

The young man fired his machine, Stihl 32-inch chainsaw, the old man knew it — rrm, rrrrmmm, rrrrmmmm — and pressed it into the tree, with his arms and his legs and his body.

The sawdust flew and he focused, stared into the cut, doing his job the best he could.

His tongue stuck out the side of his mouth. He shifted his weight, here, there, nuances, the craft, as he had been told.

Whirrr!

"Bang!"

"Aaaaah! Aah! Aah! Aaah! Aaaaaahhhh!

"Help me!"

The old man watched, felt the drops fall on the leaves around him, watched the young man flopping on his back, kicking, clawing to make things better.

And they were not.

The old man picked up his bag of spikes, placed the hammer inside the bag, threw it all over his shoulder, walked out of the brush, made a wide arc around the squirming young man, straight ahead, through the running men, the pickup radios squawking.

He stopped.

Pitched his chin to hear the sirens in town.

Headed this way.

In town, Honey White Bear-de la Rosa stopped on her way back to the office after leaving her group to watch the trail of ambulances, fire trucks and police cars roaring down main street.

Kamil K. shifted down yet lower in his seat, then raised up, went outside to stand by his car to watch the action.

Nick Green, Langley Harmsworth, the busy photographer, Fulton Crampton and Harland Lombardi paused in front of the main building to also stare at the spectacle of the frantic emergency vehicles.

"It's that time of year again!" shouted Nick.

After the loud had passed Nick suggested they walk over to the sub-title bunker. He wanted to show them the new razor wire.

"You won't believe how sharp it is!"

Reporter Randy sat in his office, late at night, the only light on all of main street his, the computer screen.

He had just returned from visting The Widow Thornpine.

His fingers and heart pumped, boomboomboomboom.

He fashioned himself something of a Tom Wolfe, Hunter Thompson, Herman Melville, or that sumbitch Cal Carstenson over at *The New Broom New Deal* who always got the awards, the interns, the grocery ads — and he was in the zone, the little pinch of whiskey in the coffee cup and the cigarette smoking in the tray.

Who Was Blaze Thornpine, Roman Empire Expert?

He looked up at a shadow across the moonlight, someone looking in the window at the dull thumping of the computer keys.

Go the schmuck away, Randy sent out a mind text.

Blaze Thornpine, in West Virginia, checking out the differences and similarities of Roman and Gothic architecture.

Hmmm.

Randy inserted subheads to go back and write something later.

Castle fire.

Roman Empire expert who converted to the Civil War when he met his wife, who was a Civil War battle reenactor along with her whole family.

When named by The History Committee as Historian Of The Year you get to choose your own scene to start the new history book production promotion schedule.

It's your funeral.

Randy smiled. He sipped, smoked, looked up at the outside, the moon.

So, after (what's his name?) was shot running out of the Ford Theater, which was "artistic history," but only .05 percent would notice and that's not enough to make a difference. The key was drama and melodrama when you could get it.

He was shot by a woman. Maybe. Or not. Perhaps.

**Who is Sonny?

Mary Todd Lincoln, who was his mistress or his wife. She dropped the weapon and walked (not knowing?) he was dead. (But) loving the cathartic release.

Randy would go back later and correct his notes.

Though that was a recurring nightmare, that the paper had gone out and he had left in his notes, with swear words and talking about some persons in town.

Someone put live ammo in the (what kind/gun) Kruzinany's — why. The feud. Kill Them All. Written on his grandfather's gravestone.

"Dude. He meant semi-colons. That was his famous saying. My father told me. Dude."

"Oh. Really?"

Intrigue, lying, conspiracy, has been in history throughout history — deceit, murder, so easy to read and ho-hum from a long ways away but not up close. Not up close. That's all this is, we are living history, and that's not as easy as it sounds. Yesterday is history, today is history, and so (is/will be) tomorrow. It's happening. Believe it.

Randy was on it (like stink on shit). He put that last part in bold so he would NOT miss it.

Who killed Blaze Thornpine?

who put ammo in gun — who pulled trigger (Beantree) — what about castle fire — accident stumbling over torches to run out as last torch extinguished.

Or what? — P.O.D., self publishing — old job wooden type.

HISTORIAN creating trouble, digging, also getting into trouble himself (Proverb)

a new broom sweeps clean.

New management will often make radical changes

Blaze Thornpine — went to college, studied Rome

West Liberty University, West Liberty, West Virginia

"Pay Attention. Be Astonished. Tell About It!"

Phi Alpha Theta

The Latin phrase 'Sic Semper Tyrannis' translates to 'thus always to tyrants' and is credited to Marcus Brutus during the assassination of Julius Caesar. The phrase is used as a motto against abuses of power and was also used by John Wilkes Booth during the assassination of President Lincoln.

From the website for the West Liberty History department:

Am I a good candidate for the History major at West Liberty?

If you are driven to understand how the world works, how it came to its present situation, and more importantly how to take the lessons of the past and apply them towards solving the problems of the future, then a degree in history might be for you. You will be required to read a variety of styles of literature, work hard, question authority, and learn how to think for yourself rather than simply repeating the information of the past. Historical scholarship requires self-discipline and a dedication to "reading between the lines" in order to uncover the hidden meaning behind authors' intentions. Furthermore, an eye for detail, a creative mind, and a desire to understand the results of human interaction are keys to success in history.

The Widow Thornpine.

Formerly Dollie Belle Lee.

They met — he was out (doing something/how studying Roman architecture in U.S.) came upon a battle — something Crossing or something Courthouse — she was (soldier, ___) fired right at him to get his attention. Was supposed to be blanks. She didn't realize. She just knew he was the one.

He liked the idea of being able to do onsite research, and he liked the idea of some day seeing Dollie Belle naked (DELETE), so switched to Civil War History. They discussed and argued about all aspects of the Civil War and Lincoln and who killed Lincoln.

He liked the idea of having a frontline history job, writing history — conferring right eye to right eye with colleagues about what should be in the books, putting it right out into so many schools, not just teaching one class in high school.

Or relatively small number of students in college.

Got master's degree in Morgantown

From the Widow Thornpine nee Lee's papers, notes of her husband's that she let this author peruse:

(stains: coffee? orange juice? tears?)

I just wonder. Why can't we talk about some things. Why not all things? Just saying, you know.

Randy sat back, satisfied with such a good start on his Thornpine piece.

He lit a new cigarette from the old one, finished the whiskey, ran his tongue around his lips, stood with the empty glass and walked to the front door.

He smelled cedar wood smoke and felt like he was a part of something. No. He was the something. He was something they had never seen before.

He stood in the door enjoying the buzz and the quiet night and the moon, exhaling the cigarette fumes like an idling old Pontiac through the screen.

The moon was the only light in town, everyone in bed, the town blacked out as if afraid of being bombed, the street lamps still a few weeks from being turned back on, as part of "the enlightenment" of The Pageant and the new sophomore history textbook.

Randy pushed his nose into the screen, closed his eyes and thought about whether to go back to work or home to bed.

"Hey."

His eyes shot open like a wild shade at the sight of another nose opposite his on the screen.

"Aaah!"

He shouted, stepped back and prepared to die.

He stepped up again, put his nose into the screen.

"Daisy?"

"I have something," she said.

"Can you open the door?"

"It's open."

He pushed it with the glass, taking a swig on the cigarette.

Daisy held out a piece of paper.

"It's from Nick," she said.

"I don't think he likes you."

"Well, I ...," said Randy as the door slapped.

He heard Daisy's quick steps on the sidewalk.

He listened for a car as he stuffed the note into his pants and mentally searched the office for more whiskey.

Finding none Randy stared at the moon, wondering a little about Blaze Thornpine, more about Dollie Belle Lee.

"Good evening, sir."

Randy dropped to the floor. He just felt he must.

His glass shattered.

He kept hold of the cigarette between two fingers like a chopsticks collector as he struggled to see who was outside the screen now.

Randy fought to his knees and wondered if the door had some kind of a schmucking latch or hook!

"You dropt sumthin."

The dark shadow now had two heads, way up high.

"Huh?" said Randy.

"Right there," said the deeper second voice.

"Oh."

He reached and picked up the unread, folded note inside the swatch of moonshine on the floor.

"Okay, thanks," said Randy, getting the note, stepping back to pull himself up by the desk, reaching back blindly, finding a stapler.

He flicked it open, like a knife, and pointed the weapon, held it out in front with both hands, along with the smoking cigarette, at the two-headed tall shadow in the screen door.

And just as quickly as it had come, the monster departed the scene, as if bored.

Randy folded the stapler gun and turned to place it on the desk.

"Who was that?"

Startled yet again, Randy hurled around, his hands up.

"Hey. I know we never ...."

"Green? That you?" said Randy.

"Yeah, I know we never got along," said Nick, the new shadow in the screen.

"But ... "

"What the schmuck are you doing!" said Randy.

"It's schmucking past midnight, man!"

"I heard you were out to see Dollie Belle," said Nick, "and so I was just wondering."

"Schmucking past midnight, man," said Randy, putting his nose right into the screen.

"Yeah, well, yeah.

"Hey, did Daisy give you a note?"

Randy shoved his nose into the screen and gritted his teeth to make Nickostatos Greenberg go away and thought to himself if he had a stapler gun right now he would shoot Nick Green.

"Well, just forget about that," said Nick.

"Can you hear me?

"That note, ya know.

"Just pitch it.

"Ya know?"

Randy fumbled and found the latch hook for the door and snapped it tight.

"Yahhh, well, anyway," said Nick as he turned and walked away.

Randy shook his head, took a deep breath, looked up at the moon.

He heard footsteps.

He watched the person walking kitty corner across the street.

"My schmucking-Jesus-Christ!" he muttered to himself.

Langley Harmsworth took long, graceful, slow strides, eyes, straight, a model on the runway, not looking either way as she crossed the street.

"I heard.

"You got the Dollie Belle Lee interview."

Her voice was so schmucking deep.

She pressed her nose and breasts firmly, steadily, gradually, continually, into the screen.

Randy found the latch and let her in.

CHAPTER TWENTY-SIX

"Perhaps we are all dupes, manipulated by elite white male capitalists who orchestrate how history is written as part of their scheme to perpetuate their own power and privilege at the expense of the rest of us."
— James W. Louwen, Lies My Teachers Told Me

Nick Green looked up.
At the hand that was handing him another note.
At the ring on the finger.
"Is that a diamond?" he asked.
Daisy pushed out the note to say, take it.
Nick took.
She drew back her hand.
"Yes," she said.
"Well, I had no idea!" he said.
"Who is the lucky guy?"
"You wouldn't know him."
"I might."
"Harland Lombardi."
"Well, that was quick!
"Well, I better get a move on, then," Nick said as he read the note.

Nick, he sweeps snow off the front steps, meets with university history professors, New York marketing firms, goes into the woods and gets only the best trees, goes to the downtown bars, has a good wife, and ten children, lives in the same home he was born in. He drinks, smokes, gambles in the back room of his favorite dive bar. There are more expensive ones, and some in the city, but he goes here.

Nick, he wants to retire and go fishing. Or, see the world, as his wife wants to, or go live in half a dozen different towns around the country as some of his children want him to.

He has one son and one daughter working at the plant. The idea is to pass it down to them. That's always been the plan.

He walks most everywhere, across campus, across town, but when he gets a chance to drive, he listens to sports talk radio and classical to escape, just like he went in the days after the attacks of Sept. 11. He did not walk anywhere for over a month, even to the warehouse or sub-title bunker.

But, big but, will there be anything left to pass down?

Nick thought about himself as he walked to meet with Honey White Bear-de la Rosa. He'd been looking at family photos late one recent night and it had put him in a self-aware stage, perhaps too self-aware, introspective, unable to move, to scratch one's own back without thinking about that one time you scratched your back, was it thirty years ago already?

They were to meet at The Old Theatre. There was also The New Theater, built more recently.

The Old, as most called it, was now mostly a storage bin for The Pageant.

Nick walked in upon the old thick red carpet, down the familiar line made by the golden rope and the wall filled with old movie posters — *Vertigo, Casablanca, Breakfast At Tiffany's, Citizen Kane, Rebel Without A Cause, 101 Dalmatians, PT 109, The Jungle Book* — where you are routed past the concession stand and then right up to the big double doors with the oversized golden handles.

He gave one a heave, jumped inside and could not see.

He felt the old incline, smelled the Sugar Babies and saw Honey White Bear-de la Rosa down on stage, climbing around on the Fort Sumter float.

The stage, from back in the vaudeville days, rotated, when it worked.

Now it twirled with the floats that depicted the chapters of the sophomore history text.

Each year they were all trucked up the cement ramp, over the dock, right here, for storage, and also, if they did get some rain, The Pageant could just be held here, bring in the people, crank the old stage around a quarter turn every few minutes or so, put on the popcorn and there ya go. You got yerself A Pageant.

Nick made his way down the aisle, touching every chair.

He got to where he would be able to startle her.

He got ready.

"I love this time of year," she said while fiddling with a pink paper chrysanthemum.

"We are almost ready."

"Yeah," he said, looking up at her, his hands on his hips, like Mickey Rooney staring up at Father Flanagan the statue.

"Well, we're going to need to postpone," said Nick.

"For awhile."

There.

He'd said it. He might sleep now.

And he might not, but this part was done finally.

Honey turned her head slightly, as if a momma bear leaning over her honey tree at a lone little buzzing bee.

She shook her head and finished with her pink flower.

She stepped down, gracefully, one foot, then the other, not one big, showy enthusiastic leap. There was time.

"We can't," she said.

"For one, your sales teams are out talking to school boards around the nation. They have rooms rented."

Before Nick could imagine, faster than his eyes and his brain could follow, Honey hopped.

She perched-posed on the edge of the stage, in her red dress, her legs crossed, eating an apple, her dream-catcher earrings dancing.

"Do it next year, Neeky."

The apple crunched and became mush in her teeth.

"We need to push forward. It's that time of year again."

"Not 'til I figure this out," he said, sticking his hands into his back pockets.

"Not until we make some changes."

He had lit the stove. He watched her boil.

She ate the core. The stem stuck out between her lips. She plucked it and flicked it.

"Changes!"

Honey uncrossed her legs, turned over and let herself down from the stage like a Rockette to stand nose to nose with Nick Green.

"What changes?"

"We have not time for your *crazy* changes. The pageant is beginning.

"Nick.

"They are lining up at the heated war memorial pool with new benches in ten days."

"Nine," he said.

"Nine!" she said.

She sat in the front row and patted the chair next to her.

"One man has died already," she said.

"Yeah," he said. "What do you think about all that?"

"I don't know," she said.

"Come. Sit."

Nick sat.

"People like to hear what they already believe, releases endorphins, that's what I've heard, a drug that makes them feel good," she said.

"If they hear something they don't already agree with, they turn it off.

"That's why it's so important to install certain wiring, beliefs when they are young.

"It makes it very difficult or impossible to change when they get older.

"Only by a major effort could that ever happen, even with one person.

"That's what we want.

"Neeeeky, that's what we all want.

"That's why the sssschmucking pageant is so sssschmucking goddamned-important," she said, whispering in his ear.

"Nick."

She brushed his leg with her hand.

At least he thought she had.

CHAPTER TWENTY-SEVEN

"Nations are not communities and never have been. The history of any country, presented as the history of a family, conceals the fierce conflicts of interest (sometimes exploding, often repressed) between conquerors and conquered, masters and slaves, capitalists and workers, dominators and dominated in race and sex. And in such as world of conflict, a world of victims and executioners, it is the job of thinking people, as Albert Camus suggested, not to be on the side of the executioners."
— *Howard Zinn*, A People's History of the United States: 1492 to Present

Nick moseyed as he had never moseyed down the sidewalk on his way back from his meeting with Honey White Bear-de la Rosa.

He rolled by The Passed Time Bakery and saw Deanno sitting in the one window table.

Deanno waved. Nick went inside.

"Hey."

Nick sat.

With a pointer finger Deanno pushed over one of his Pre-History Cakes.

"Little dry," said Deanno in a whisper.

Nick began peeling the paper.

"Thanks. Hey, is that, umm, that, umm ...?

"Limbaugh?"

"McKinley."

"Hey, when *is* The Sub-Title Banquet?" said Nick.

Deanno, his mouth full, nodded up to "The Sub-Title Banquet, History Pageant, Celebrity Softball Tournament" poster on the window, which neither of them could read backwards, but anyway.

Deanno choked down his cupcake, folded his red paper cup, pushed away from the table, stood, fired the paper toward the open plastic garbage can.

"Umm, soon," he said, on his way out.

Outside, Nick looked back at the big four-color poster that had been the subject over the winter of so freeking many meetings to publicize everything in the annual "You're History Days" in New Town:

The Naming of The Historian Of the Year & Shootout, Pre-History Cupcake Sale, The Sub-Title Banquet, Celebrity Softball Tournament, The Sophomore History Bee, Dust Bowl Treasure Hunt, All-Town Moon Rock Scavenger Hunt, The History Pageant & Chamber Dunk Tank, The Shoshone Gravesite Annual Dig, then finally THE Big Delivery Truck All-Town Send Off & Popcorn Cook-Off.

In tiny type that someone had insisted on, it read:

Artifacts tell their own stories.
Artifacts connect people.
Artifacts mean many things.
Artifacts capture moments.
Artifacts reflect changes.

"Weirdos," Nick muttered, turned and bumped right into the laughing Randy the reporter and Langley Harmsworth. He quickly noted how strange the word "artifact" sounded when you said it over and over and over.

"Who's weird?" said Randy as he chained the bicycle built for two to the only parking meter in town.

They bumped shoulders, swung their hands, laced together.

"We're grabbing a Pre-History Cake," said Langley Harmsworth. "It's that time of year."

She showed Nick quickly the front page of *The Journal-Times*, again the big color photo of the dead Blaze Thornpine, the banner five column headline: "Dollie Belle Lee-Thornpine Talks", by Randy, editor; Langley Harmsworth.

"Oh, nice," said Nick.

He grabbed it by a corner and pulled it close. He squinted.

Did it look like Thornpine was winking, one eye open, just a bit?

"Join us?"

"We've got some questions," said Randy, "take just a minute?"

"Nah, I was just," said Nick. "Prob'ly some other time, huh?"

He side-stepped to let them past.

"Suit yourself," whispered Langley Harmsworth.

The tiny bell jingled out their entrance.

Their juvenile giggles were kindly swallowed by the door.

Nick cranked his mosey into a stride, and then almost a trot as he began to need to use the restroom.

The long campus block, the long, long hedge, was almost too much for him to bear. The shuttle bus beeped as Nick jogged across the drive in front of it and waved.

He passed Fulton and Harland sitting on the cement bench outside the main office.

He waved.

Harland waved back.

Nick stopped and said congratulations to Harland.

"Thanks," said Harland.

"That was quick," said Nick.

"We've actually been texting for over a month," said Harland.

"Well, way to go," said Nick.

"Thanks," said Harland.

"No problem," said Nick, leaning and reaching to take a swipe at patting Harland on the shoulder and coming up short.

Nick turned to charge inside, stopped quick and turned.

"When is the big event?"

"We thought the day of the pageant would be cool."

"Nice, good idea. That should be no problem. No problem at all."

Nick hurried.

He ran past Daisy holding up a piece of paper into Hess Bangor's office, grabbed him by the arm and dragged him down the hall to the restroom.

Nick hustled Hess Bangor inside, pushed him toward the end stall and grabbed the middle one.

"Woah," he said.

Nick sensed Bobby Barkham in the first stall.

"What can you tell me?" said Nick.

"About what?" said Bobby Barkham.

"About anything," said Nick.

"I need some answers."

"About what?"

"Anything. Hess, you here?"

Hess flushed.

"That's Hess," said Nick.

"I know Hess," said Bobby.

"Oh, yeah, of course," said Nick.

"Hey, Bobby," said Hess.

"Hess," said Bobby Barkham.

"When?" said Nick.

"Your answers."

"Yeah," said Nick.

"Well, first I probably should know the questions."

"When?" said Bobby Barkham.

The door opened.

They sensed someone standing there, holding the door open, with tilted head, trying to see shoes, thinking, "What the hell! No room!"

"Kamil," said Nick.

"Close the door, huh?"

The person left in a huff it seemed.

The door closed slowly, on its own.

"So Hess," said Nick.

"Any interestin' readin' over there?"

"Some," said Hess.

"What'd he say?" said Bobby Barkham.

"He said some," said Nick.

"What's that mean?" said Bobby Barkham.

"Beats me," said Nick.

"What's that mean, Hess?"

Hess flushed again.

Nick told Bobby Barkham he needed those answers of the important questions that he needed to know ASAP, and leaving Hess Bangor where he was, got up, washed his hands, blew dried them perfunctorily and left.

Nick took out his new cellphone and worked to send Daisy a text to tell The Generals to gather for a meeting as he headed for The Warehouse.

He saw Eddie sitting on a forklift, his back to the door. Nick stalked toward him.

"Hey!" he grabbed Eddie by the shoulders.

Eddie looked surprised as Nick stuck his head around.

Nick saw he was working on something, a hand-sized notebook in his lap.

"Whatcha doin'?" said Nick.

"Nothin'," said Eddie, snatching up the notebook as any artist not used to showing his work would possibly do.

Nick grabbed the notebook playfully out of Eddie's hands.

"Hey!" said Eddie.

"That's mine! Give it."

He reached in vain as Nick danced away, opening the notebook, looking inside as an annoying younger brother finding a diary in the tree house.

Eddie stopped reaching as Nick stopped laughing and dancing. He stared at the notebook.

"It's familiar," he said.

"My God.

"I've seen this before, where have I seen this before?

"Eddie?"

"Nowhere, boss, jus' lemme have it.

"Please?"

"Oh, sure, sure, sure," said Nick.

He hurried back to the forklift where Eddie still sat, gave Eddie his book and headed out from whence he had come.

"I thought Daisy said about a meetin'!" Eddie yelled after him.

Nick kept walking, waving one hand up over his head.

Nick walked across the yard, downtown, up the hill, toward the school.

He passed the mini-golf mini-park and the pond and did not see the old man sitting in one of The Nine Big Trees, which the name represented something, whittling what might have been a 27-ounce pool stick or a spear.

At the four-way Nick crossed diagonally toward the school, then in the middle of the road cut back, over to Janey's house.

CHAPTER TWENTY-EIGHT

"What struck me as I began to study history was how nationalist fervor — inculcated from childhood on by pledges of allegiance, national anthems, flags waving and rhetoric blowing — permeated the educational system of all countries, including our own. I wonder how the foreign policies of the United States would look if we wiped out the national boundaries of the world, at least in our minds, and thought of all the children everywhere as our own. Then we could never drop an atomic bomb on Hiroshima or napalm on Vietnam, or wage war anywhere, because wars, especially in our time, are always wars against children, indeed our children."
— Howard Zinn, A People's History of the United States: 1492 to Present

As he pushed through the gate Nick kept an eye on the note on the front porch door.

"We Are Dead," it said, written in a child's crayon handwriting with crude drawings of children standing up with "X's" for eyes.

Cautiously he pushed inside.

He saw Able's neat corner, took one more step to look closer. If he was there he was hiding really great.

Then another note on the door leading to the living room.

"The Undead."

More drawings of children flat on their back, lying down, floating.

Inside, on the bedroom doors, bathroom, kitchen, more drawings of dead in all conceivable stick figure poses.

On the white board calendar Nick saw that apparently the dead and undead were now at the All-Town Sophomore History Bee and Ice Cream Social in the Forum in City Park.

Nick wanted to see Able's sophomore American history book.

He went to the porch, found the book and sat deep in the old sofa.

And there it was, right inside the cover.

The same words, same drawing that Eddie had been working on.

"How ... in-the ... hell?" Nick said out loud.

He ran out the door, through the gate, across the street.

His shoes clicked up the high school steps.

He heard footsteps behind him.

A ghost perhaps, a Civil War ghost such as Dollie Belle Lee had expounded upon in her most recent interview in "The Journal-Times Dollie Belle Lee Interview Series."

He waited for the ghost to catch him if it wanted.

The steps grew louder.

The ghost, dressed as an Indian maiden, approached him, head down, and stopped one step below him.

"Where are the children?" Nick asked.

"Ohhhh," said the ghost.

"That g'damn hist'ry bee."

"Oh, hey, Miss Principal! How's it hangin'?"

Nick asked if he might take a quick look in his daughter's room.

"Of course," she said as if that was precisely the reason she was here.

She let him in and sat on the floor, fanning her face with her feather as Nick looked inside desks, locker, behind the aquarium, under Christmas wrapping paper in his daughter's desk for the sophomore American History textbooks.

He flipped each one open, then the next, the next.

"I don't understand," he said, shouting across the room.

"So. Now you know," she said.

"Know what?"

"You see the note, the drawing."

"But, why do I know something ... from that?"

"You just do. Don't you see?"

She said that it was time for her to be getting back and that he must leave and neither one of them was ever there.

Nick and Miss Principal nodded solemnly, bonding them for life, as they parted on the front sidewalk.

* * *

He squinted as he entered the side door, feeling in front and on the side like a blind man, smelling cigarettes and beer. He grinned at the ol' familiar feeling, his shoes sticking to the floor.

It had been a long time since he'd been in The Baskerville, not since it was The Garamond and "bye, bye Miss American Pie" played on the radio, not since that night that he swore he'd never return.

In the corner, he sat there, as if he'd never left, The John Brown, dealing Skip-Bo to old ladies dressed in bonnets, who had slipped out of the History Bee for some real action it seemed.

Many years ago, on an early summer night like this, Nick Green and The John Brown had met in The Baskerville nee Garamond.

Oh what a night.

They had come there after a softball game, after a pop fly to short left field had been dropped, stayed too long, and though the details were not clear, it had been bad, very bad, and they had never spoken of it, because they did not remember, just that it had been bad.

"So," John Brown shouted.

"We meet again.

"Finally.

"As we must."

"I did see you in the cafeteria."

"Me too."

"Yeah, well ... yeah," said Nick as he walked over to stand and watch the game.

"You got a minute?"

With a wave of his hand John Brown sent the old ladies scurrying to play pinball.

He slammed an empty plastic container of One Calorie Lime-Grape Kool-Aid on the table and demanded another.

Nick told him about the notes inside all of the history books, and how he thought Eddie had put them there.

He showed him a history book he had stuck down the front of his pants while Principal Miss Bordeaux apparently watched closely.

The note was in blue pen, printed, on the title page:

History Is So Boring.
Teachers just go throo the motions. And then there was a drawing of a superhero firing laser beams or spider webs from its hands.

Pres'dents Book of Secrets
Platoz Cave.

He asked why.

"What does all that shit mean?" said Nick, throwing back his Kool-Aid.

John Brown pointed out the obvious misspellings perhaps meant to throw any investigator off the scent and put a big finger on "Pres'dent's Book of Secrets."

"That's interesting," he said.

"I know, right?" said Nick.

"I know what that schmucking is," said John Brown.

"I found it on Scoop.It, it's a schmucking website finder thing, under 'conspiracies.'"

He made air quotes while keeping the shot glass in one hand.

Nick shoved his shot glass to the middle of the table, keeping his eyes on John Brown.

John Brown drank the Kool-Aid with Nick Green straight away, slamming 1.5 ounce shots until their arms got tired.

John Brown said what? why? Would you ever think I would understand what those notes mean? What does that have to do with Margins & Spacing or Focus Groups, neither of which have any control over what goes on the first title pages.

Are you daft, man!

"Are you out of yer mind?

"Though.

"And sometimes, maybe every hundred years or so, someone gets the idea that history is not important. We can live with these books for another five or ten years and besides, it's boring. Our parents don't care about it. The kids sure don't. And even the history teachers are starting to think maybe something more relevant to the lives of the students, like maybe bird calls or face painting would be money better spent.

"And The Pres'dent's Book of Secrets."

"I was wondering when you were," said Nick.

"It's a book that is passed down from President to President, like a diary. It tells about UFOs and who killed what with who and where. It's where we got The Game of Clue, some say. Others don't think so. They think something else."

"Oh, I see. How would anyone know that?" said Nick.

"You know, if it's a secret."

"I do not know," said John Brown.

"Seeee, there ya go. Yer right on top of it, champ."

"Well," said Nick.

And that's all he said, setting his shot glass down gently.

The John Brown had just been someone who sounded like he knew things when they were in high school, but now maybe not so much, but not wanting to hurt his feelings, Nick just set down the shot glass, waved the old ladies back over to their Skip-Bo game and walked out the side door, which was also the back door, there not being any back door.

CHAPTER TWENTY-NINE

Sic semper tyrannis is a Latin phrase meaning "thus always to tyrants." The full quotation is Sic semper evello mortem tyrannis (literally: "Thus always I eradicate tyrants' lives"), "death to tyrants" or "down with the tyrant." The phrase is often said to have originated with Marcus Junius Brutus during the assassination of Julius Caesar, but according to Plutarch, Brutus either did not have a chance to say anything, or if he did, no one heard what was said:

"Caesar thus done to death, the senators, although Brutus came forward as if to say something about what had been done, would not wait to hear him, but burst out of doors and fled, thus filling the people with confusion and helpless fear ...

"The phrase has been invoked historically in Europe and other parts of the world as an epithet or rallying cry against abuse of power. In the United States it is best known as the words John Wilkes Booth shouted during his assassination of President Abraham Lincoln."

— Wikipedia

In the meantime.

Daisy prepared for her marriage to Harland Lombardi.

On her breaks she now sat with Harland Lombardi and Fulton Crampton on the front cement bench without a backrest ordering triangle

119

sandwiches on her cellphone and folding napkins, setting them gently into a cardboard book box on the sidewalk.

While, in the meantime, in the cafeteria, the gluers sat on their side, wearing their brand new Union #374 caps and shirts, holding their signs, "Nothing Exists! You Are Sooo Stupid!" while the historians, in period garb, sat on the other side of the big, wide, long, cement block wall room holding their signs, "History Is What WE Say It Is !!! Geez."

All through the lunch hour they fired grape shot at each other, white, red, with seeds, without. Some fell short, some splattered on the wall or the cooks behind them, some were caught in the hand and eaten or fired right back.

Nick heard some of that through an open door somewhere as he passed The New Mini-Golf Park and the pond to The Nine Big Trees.

He looked up and saw the dangling feet of the old man.

Wood chips and shavings floated down, into Nick's eyes, onto his hair and his shoes.

He looked for handholds, footholds.

He hugged the tree and shinnied. He slid down. He was too short, too stubby, too old. The tree was too hard, too slick, too fat.

The old man fired a chunk down at Nick, glancing it off his shoulder.

Nick looked up.

The old man nodded to the back of the tree, where Nick found the old wooden ladder that had been missing for a few months or years from the warehouse.

Nick climbed, straight up.

The ladder got him to the first branch.

In a half hour he had made it to the third branch where he sat gingerly next to the old man, still whittling.

"Eddie said I could use it. You can ask ..."

"Yeah, but it's got to go back," said Nick.

"Eddie runs the warehouse," said the old man.

"I would think if he really needed ...."

The old man cut himself off and dug his knife into his stick.

Nick stuck out his hand to shake.

"Do you work for me?" he said.

The old man looked at Nick's hand and back to his whittling what might have been a 27-ounce pool stick or a spear.

"You work for me, son."

Nick had figured as much.

Eddie's father. Emil Beantree.

He'd heard stories.

About how he had risen from humble beginnings to one of the owners of the publishing house, fallen into bad graces, studied with the Baha Ba Yami over in Junction City, and gone to the woods to fight.

And that he was a murderer, an insurgent, if one wanted to look at it all from that particular angle. A woods savior, a freedom fighter, if you wanted to take that approach.

Well, Nick thought, since he was up here.

And he asked him the same things that he had been asking everyone.

He got back pretty much the same answers that had come from John Brown in between Skip-Bo games over shots of red Kool-Aid.

And sometimes, maybe every hundred years or so, someone gets the idea that history is not important. We can live with these books for another five or ten years and besides, it's boring. Our parents don't care about it. The kids sure don't. And even the history teachers are starting to think maybe something more relevant to the lives of the students, like maybe bird calls or face painting would be money better spent.

Nick told him about the notes inside all of the history books, and how he thought Eddie had put them there.

He showed him. Set a history book he had stuck down the front of his pants when Principal Miss Bordeaux was looking if not staring.

"How did she not notice that?" said the old man.

Nick shrugged.

The note was in blue pen, printed, on the title page:

History Is So Boring.

Teachers just go throo the motions.

And then there was as we know, the drawing of a superhero firing laser beams or spider webs from its hands.

Pres'dents Book of Secrets

Platoz Cave.

The old man's head began to tilt contemplatively and so Nick checked his watch. He felt a story coming on and he didn't have time, but he was thirty feet up.

The old man told Nick that he kills young loggers.

"I used to be a young man, a logger," he said.

"I thought you were a self-taught accountant," said Nick.

"Then I became an owner," the old man continued.

"And then I became an eagle."

Nick reached his toes for the ladder and felt all around him.

Nick let the old man tell about being an eagle and soaring and the river and the wind and the sun and moon and Pluto and all that shit that old men in trees will tell when the ladder is not super close.

The old man took a breath and Nick asked him all about all the shit that was on his mind.

The Book of Secrets.

The death of Blaze Thornpine.

What should I tell Fulton Crampton?

How to sell history books.

What should be in the pageant.

Should there even be history books.

"Now is the time. If you have anything to say to me, now is the time."

Nick finished up, starting to reach for some way to get the schmuck down.

"Yes," said the old man.

"Who are you?"

"You don't know me?"

"Have I seen you fishing?"

"No," said Nick.

Oh, brother, he thought, here we go again, up into the clouds.

"Well, gotta go, seeya."

He just then noticed feathers in the old man's hair, between his fingers and one in his toes.

"Some things are nice," said the old man.

"Some things are not nice.

"Some things are battles. Knock-down, drag-out.

"Decide which things are nice and which are battles.

"And if you can't decide, until you can decide, maybe go fishing."

"Aaaaand that-also-makes-no-sense ... so schmucking Braveheart," grumbled Nick.

"The schmucking fish in the river, and the moon eats the fish, bleh, bleh, bleh. And becomes the schmucking eagle."

He mumbled to himself as he searched for a way down.

Nick balanced on the branch, both hands on the trunk, trying to remember how he ever got there from the ladder.

"So, dude, old dude. You're an eagle, huh?"

The old man, seeing the doubt and the irony and sarcasm and weariness in Nick's eyes, smiled softly and chuckled, to himself, and stroked another stroke on his pool cue or spear.

"Yep," he said.

"I am that is."

Now he's schmucking Yoda, thought Nick. How the schmuck do I get out of here!

Nick climbed down, thought about whether the ladder needed to go back to the warehouse, but then, how would the old man get down?

He heard a screech, looked up, and saw an eagle circling, looking down.

CHAPTER THIRTY

Comment section on website:
Bonnie [ ] says:
APRIL 19, 2014 AT 9:09 AM
"Thank you for providing another thought-provoking & in-depth report of this incident.
"I remember questioning the "official explanation" at the time (when I was still in high school) & how we secretly passed around the "Zapruder Report" like it was stolen Russian intelligence & the FBI would storm our houses. Then a couple of yrs. later seeing Ruby shoot Oswald on live TV, I always felt there was more to this than was being offered.
"We citizens of the United States have to thread our way through a dangerous minefield of information, picking out what is true from what is not true. The "mainstream media" has the vaunted position it does precisely because it is controlled by intelligence interests. Those news outlets which are not so controlled are suppressed (and belittled) before the true version of events can get traction."

"So, we meet again," said Nick, holding the door for Randy and Langley Harmsworth coming out of the new office for Martha and Mary. They nodded, unsmiling, seeming to be in a hurry.

Nick found Martha and Mary seated side by side along their same old big knotty oak table.

He smelled new carpet and incense, maybe marijuana? Maybe alfalfa?

Martha and Mary were hunched over pieces of parchment, elbows on the ends to keep them from curling. Two computers bracketed them, askew, as if having been pushed away.

"So," said Nick.

They looked up.

Martha leaned to spit and Nick hoped they'd brought over the Folger's can.

"How's the old blogging, desktop publishing, social media marketing coming?" he said.

Vending machines filled the back wall. The big windows looked out onto the ninth tee. The ceiling featured a slanted, tinted glass.

"Having a little delay getting started on all that," said Mary.

"Yeah," said Martha, spitting again.

"Not as far along as we'd like to be at this point," said Mary.

They heard yelling, hollering, screaming, chanting coming from the cafeteria.

"Wow, what a deal," said Nick.

"S'pose I should go over there, huh?"

"Nonsense," said Mary.

She opened a Skoal tin by slicing it with a long purple fingernail, held it out to offer to Nick. He put up a hand and shook his head.

She put a three-finger wad into her lower lip, spit at what could be the floor and also could be the Folger's can.

She put up a finger to say she had something to say and offered the can to Nick.

He shook his head.

Martha pushed back and headed to the vending machines wall.

"It's a ruse," said Mary.

"The whole gluers and historians strike and protests. That's all it is."

"No it's not," said Nick.

"They are pretty mad. But I can't do anything about it. It's all soooo ... freekin ... esoteric. We do not exist. History is what we say it is. Yeah, okay, well, whatever, but we've got to produce a history book that someone will use, and sell it or we don't get food and lives. That's current history that I'm pretty sure does exist."

Nick looked all around for a chair, and finding none, sat on the floor at a distance from the table that he could see Mary's head, now Martha as she sat with her Twix and Twizzlers.

"Yeah, but," said Mary.

She bit into the plastic and put a finger into the air.

"It is all run by Fulton Crampton, Harland Guy and The Big Boss in New York."

She made air quotes with two Twizzlers around "The Big Boss."

"Don't trust Daisy Doorknob," said Mary in a rush as if she had been wanting to say it for a long time.

She held out the Twizzler pack to offer to Nick.

"Yeah, okay," he said, pushed up to his knees, crawled to the table, drew out a thick red string and fell back to his almost cozy spot.

"Es-pe-cially."

"The Doorknors are one of our most prominent underground families," said Nick.

"A diversion, Neeky, hon'," said Martha.

"From the real issues," said Mary.

Nick leaned back on his hands, crossed his legs at the ankles.

"Is that what you told *them*?" he said, nodding at the door.

"What real issues?"

Dying to make air quotes, but not wanting to move, he just stayed as he was.

"Oh, no," said Martha.

"Those two are crazy. They really are."

"Crazed by love, stars in their eyes," said Mary.

"They are only interested in Blaze T. and Dollie Belle. We told them ... I forget. What did we tell them, M?" said Martha.

Mary spit a mixture of brown and red.

Under the table, Nick saw a line connected from Mary to the Folger's can and pumped his fist.

He curled his toes inside his new black publishers work boots, "perfect for the office and the warehouse," Daisy had found on Amazon. He closed his eyes, took a deep breath.

"We told them to go check out ... hmm," said Mary.

"Anyway, they think it's all connected, you, the parade, the sub-title, the cover, Honey, a big conspiracy, the publisher in the pantry with the pruning knife a.k.a. box cutters."

"They said, oh, god! Somebody's killing the historians of New Town! And we said, yes, they are, Herodotus, Boorstin, Zinn, Thornpine.

"And then we sent them up to the cemetery to look for the graves. And if they don't find them, then, see, look how far 'they' are willing to go to hide it all."

"Yeah, I know, right?" said Nick.

"What are the real issues?"

He successfully made air quotes around real issues and then got his hands back behind him before he hit his head on the stone floor.

Is it Blaze Thornpine?

Is it the Old Man in the Tree?

Is it Kamil patrolling main street as if it were East Berlin?

"It, what? Like what?"

"What is it?"

"What are you looking to be it, Neeky?

"Umm, it like in the answer, duuhh.

"Real."

"Please, Nickostatos. This is your office, but don't be rude," said Mary.

"Or the question?" Martha interjected.

"Yes, even the question," he said. "If I could just find out what the question is. I asked Barkham, that's not goin' anywhere.

"It like the question would be so great."

"Oh, him," said Martha. "He's crazy."

"Is that it?"

"What is it?" said Mary.

"Is it John Brown in the cafeteria?" said Nick.

"Is it Daisy with the note in the men's restroom?

"Dollie Belle Lee in the pasture with the pastor?"

"No," said Mary. "Those are just things that have happened."

"Some things happen," said Martha.

"Just happen."

"This self publishing is not such a bad deal."

Mary grabbed one of the instructional manuals from the top of a computer.

"You ought to try it. You might not get rich, but then again if you've got something you want to say, that you feel you simply must say."

"But we are a publishing house, one of the most powerful publishing houses in the entire country!" said Nick.

"Oh, yes, of course you are, dearie," said Martha.

"Of course you are," said Mary.

"Still, you might consider, considering."

Considering?

Considering what?

Considering what!

"Well, for one, Fulton is not here to try to buy from you," said Mary.

"Harland is not his muscle," said Martha.

"You must see them in a new light, a new light, dearie, a new liiiight, good night," said Mary.

"Oh, right, everybody tells me things, and not half of it's worth listening to anyway," said Nick.

"Riiighht, we know," said Martha.

And with that the lights went out, 'cept for the vending machines and the one slanted window skylight that encased the full white moon over the shining, shimmering river.

"They say they want to buy you out."

Mary and Martha said at once.

"You go 'head," said Mary.

"No, you," said Martha.

Mary spit and looked at Nick and not seeing him, stood to see Nick on his side on the floor, his knees curled to his chest, pain in his face, his hands in fists, clutched to his chest.

As the EMT's wheeled Nick Green through the The New Office glass front double doors and Randy flashed photos and Langley Harmsworth tried to get statements from the EMTs — Mary and Martha leaned over the gurney, very close to both of Nick's ears, whispering, making air quotes, hurrying along, cognizant of the crunch of time and space that would occur at the double glass doors — while Langley Harmsworth reached at the last moment to try to get her recorder in there and nodded at Randy to hurry the schmuck up and get the money shot.

The front page black and white photo ran in Wednesday's paper: Nick Green being shoved balding head-first out of the double-glass doors, barely taking up half of the gurney, his Yankees cap at his side, his publishing boots sticking out at the end of the thin, white sheets, two industrial push brooms framing the doors, Martha and Mary just barely visible, back in the shadows, backlit by the warm hum and glow of the vending machines.

CHAPTER THIRTY-ONE

"False flag operations and assassinations are a central component of the elaborate psychological warfare campaign waged on the American public to justify the so-called "global war on terrorism," and the events of September 11, 2001 are this project's cornerstone.

"Major U.S. news outlets turn a blind eye to a wide array of evidence "that Western covert operators were behind" events such as "Bali, Madrid, London 7/7, mosque bombings in Iraq and elsewhere and, of course, 9/11. Because the mainstream media are integral to the Industrial Military Academic Intelligence Media complex," journalist Barrie Zwicker observes, "the cold-blooded technicians of death face no journalistic scrutiny. Without moral, legal, technical or financial constraints, the black operators range freely, executing the orders of the global oligarchies."

— James F. Tracy

Nick lay in bed.

Harland and Fulton and Daisy sat in a line in his room, folding napkins, setting the completed ones in a box at their feet.

A nurse checked his temp, adjusted something that might have needed adjusting, headed out.

Nick opened his eyes, remembered where he was, looked for a moment at the ballgame on the TV up in the corner, then raised his left hand as high as the metal bed frame, rested his hand by the I.D. bracelet, and pointed a weak finger at Harland Lombardi.

"Why are you here?" he said.

"Well, Daisy thought ...," said Harland.

"No, not that," said Nick.

"Not here-here, but here."

Fulton Crampton shook his head and smirked.

Daisy folded faster, looked away from Nick to Harland to the television, back to the pressing napkin work in her lap.

"I came to marry Miss Daisy," said Harland, plowing through Nick's shaking head.

"I knew about her by text. Now I know her by heart."

He looked at Daisy, smiled and squeezed her hand.

"Fulton Crampton is here for other reasons."

Harland, thinking the little speech had put him in the clear, returned his attention to his folding and the ballgame on the TV up in the corner of the single hospital room.

"Yeah, yeah, yeah," wheezed Nick.

"Martha, Mary ... "

"The whiches," said Fulton Crampton.

"They are nice!"

Daisy took a swipe in Fulton Crampton's direction.

"How can I sell to you if you already own us?" said Nick to Fulton, Harland, Daisy, anyone who was listening.

"Oh, so you ... Well, then ... You are not performing. You must perform," said Fulton Crampton. "Or get out."

"Like a seal?"

"Like an employee."

"But I didn't know I was an employee, schmuck-nuts."

"I still don't believe it.

"Tell me."

Fulton Crampton half-stood to reach the remote control on Nick's bed. He pointed and changed from the game to a police show.

Nick thought about complaining ... and did not.

He set a hand on his leg to wave to the women and two children rising from the chairs on the opposite side of the room preparing to leave, saying goodbye.

"Okay, thanks then, see ya now," said Nick.

"Who was that?" said Harland.

"His ...," began Daisy before she caught herself.

"My family," said Nick.

"Oh, part of it. There's more at home. Kids. Just the one wife.

"These two work at the plant. They want me to pass it all down to them when it's time. When I'm done. Maybe I'm done now."

"Where?" said Fulton Crampton.

"Where?" said Nick.

"Where do they work? In the plant," said Fulton Crampton.

Daisy looked at Nick. Nick looked at Daisy. Daisy opened her mouth. No sound.

"Umm," said Nick.

"I'm not totally sure, somewhere. I guess I'll have to ask," he said, looking at Daisy, who was making ad-hoc sign language.

She made triangles and swirly things and a "T" and an "S" by curving her pointer finger.

Nick looked at her curiouser and curiouser.

"Oh," he said.

"Somewhere, doesn't mind, I'll find out.

"Anywaaay."

"Hard Working Americans," said Fulton Crampton.

"That is what the sub-title will be."

"There are microphones in the moose that go right back to New York," he said.

"They've been there for years. We know everything."

Daisy caught Nick's eye.

"I knew that," said Nick.

"Right?"

He looked at Daisy.

She nodded extremely subtly.

"The old fool in the tree you were talking to?" said Fulton Crampton.

"He's one of ours, a provocateur. Makes people hate tree-huggers. That's to our advantage. Why has no one ever tracked him down, put him in jail?"

"Noooo," said Nick.

"I just talked to him. He's a good guy."

"Ohhh," said Fulton Crampton.

"Everyone is good, for awhile, or for a moment, but not forever. The same with the words strong, brave. Try to be for every hour of your life and you will find yourself horribly disappointed. I'm afraid. The old man is in fact Emil Cyprus Beantree II, one of the first owners."

"Yep, yer big New York Boss threatened them all. They wouldn't sell.

"That's why we have all of what we have, in this valley, this town," said Nick.

"Beantree, Barkham, Bangor … Krusinanskys."

Fulton Crampton said the names as if they each tasted like poop on a stick at the state fair.

"And the Greeeenberrrgs," he said.

"The line of managers."

"Owners," said Nick.

"Have it your way," said Fulton Crampton.

"But you are coming to see and appreciate the power of the written word? And why we can't have you just doing whatever you want."

"I do whatever I want," said Nick, pushing on the bed to sit up.

"Nobody tells me what to do."

"Yes, of course you do," said Fulton Crampton.

Nick pointed to the door as straight as he could with the tubes on his arm.

"I think you need to leave, now."

"Information is everything," said Fulton Crampton.

"Pretty much the ballgame."

He stood, snatched the remote, pointed it at the tiny TV, and switched back to baseball.

"There are conspiracies. Everywhere."

Fulton Crampton stood at the bed, close to Nick.

"Powerful people. Everywhere. In history. In your life." –

"If you don't …"

"If I don't, what!" said Nick, snatching back the remote.

"The possibilities are endless," said Fulton Crampton, "but, just say for one example, we dig up old emails, girlfriends, videos, things of that nature. Present them to your wife, son, daughter, the local paper.

"How much fun would your life be at that point? You would kill yourself, and it wouldn't take long, you'd be surprised. And we would win.

"Will. Win."

"I heard they did not sell. They passed it on to my grandfather because he was good," said Nick.

"He was good."

"Well, you heard wrong, Nickostatos.

"They did sell. Need to know, right? You didn't. You own nothing. The old ownership doesn't exist. We have been running this from day one. It's just that … we just heard."

"You weren't playin' ball, that's all," said Harland Lombardi, pushing off to stand next to Fulton Crampton as Daisy began to pack things up.

"We're just here to clear up the misunderstanding," said Harland.

"Hard Working Americans," said Fulton Crampton.

"Remember. Remember."

Fulton Crampton pointed a finger back at Nick as he followed the others out the door, then nodded to Kamil K. and Honey White Bear-de la Rosa, with something like tears in her eyes and wearing a tight, black dress and black scarf, black fingernails.

She hurried over to him.

"Sooo, Neeeky, howz it goingk, darlingk?"

CHAPTER THIRTY-TWO

"It may be true that you can't fool all the people all the time, but you can fool enough of them to rule a large country."

— Will Durant

Honey stayed for twenty minutes, talking about The Pageant and how the Mount Rushmore float would again be the big main attraction that everyone was waiting to see again.

Nick listened with one ear while watching the ballgame and also Kamil sitting with folded arms over by the window, the sun coming through so that Nick could not really see his face.

"Don't screw this up!"

Honey pointed at Nick with a long black finger as she pranced through the door.

"We love you! Hugs! Hugs!

"You got to do the sub-title banquet and the pageant, all nice, like always," she shouted from the hall.

"And life goes on like ... normal!

"But not on time because you are taking so loon ...!"

Her voice was swallowed up by a nurse rattling a cart down the hall.

"You playing in the softball thing?" said Kamil.

He scooted his chair over, making a series of screeches that drew one, now another angry nurse head in the doorway.

"Yep," said Nick.

"I won't miss it. I'm feelin' fine."

"An old wine," said Kamil, "jus' gettin' better, huh?"

"Not really," said Nick.

"But it's the one fun thing about this whole hysterical celebration."

He made air quotes around celebration, by raising his bent wrists from the bed.

"Who controls the present controls the past," said Kamil.

"Yeah, I know," said Nick.

"Or something like that, right?"

"No, really," said Kamil.

"We heard all that from the hall. That's what he's doing, just by getting you to put out the same old history book. I finally figured it all out, thought I'd let you know, you know?"

"I looked at one, a bunch, over in the school," said Nick. "They're schmucking huge."

"Just get through it," said Nick.

"No drama, only melodrama."

"I know, right?" said Nick.

"Something's missing."

"A whole lot missing, I would say," said Kamil.

"The United States overcame these obstacles.

"Be a good citizen.

"The optimistic approach."

"Seek not to arouse parents," said Nick.

"President's Book Of Secrets," said Kamil. "That's kind of interesting."

"You saw that, too?" said Nick.

"Yup."

"Eddie puts it there. He said once he thought we should just make some shit up to help sales.

"It's the tradition that the warehouse manager is the last one to touch the books, gives them his imprimatur, his autograph, inspection, marks as inspected by Eddie," said Nick.

"Why Eddie do that? said Kamil.

He pointed right at Nick.

"His old man's that crazy guy who they say kills loggers! That's him!"

"Yeah, I don't know," said Nick. "I'll ask him. I'm going over there, hmmm, when I get out of here."

He looked around the room, at the flowers, the TV, the white.

"Textbook gaffes make news. And then you fix them and you're a hero," said Nick.

"Yup," said Kamil.

They watched two baseball reporters on the sports network arguing about something, maybe baseball.

Nick pointed the remote.

"They have millions of viewers, daily. And they are serious about who they are, what they do."

"Ah heard that," said Kamil.

"Many Americans believed that Martians attacked New York City because of a radio drama," said Nick.

"War of the Worlds," said Kamil.

"The Mouse That Roared," I like that book, said Nick.

"The Russians Are Coming, The Russians Are Coming," said Kamil. I saw that movie. I think maybe twice.

"Make up some shit," said Nick.

"Yup," said Kamil.

A nurse, with her ponytail bouncing like a prize pampered pony pranced in, checked Nick's gauges and pumps and wires, turned down the sound on the television, and handed him an already opened envelope.

Nick pulled out the card with a picture of Yoda, his favorite Star Wars character.

Get Soon Well, I Hope You Will.

"Well. I hope you are happy. That's the main deal, as we all approach the end. Have fun, be happy, enjoy your friends.

Catch you later.

love,

Mickostatos"

Nick, feeling Kamil's eyes, held up the card.

"From Meeck," he said.

"Oh. Yeah," said Kamil, looking back at the TV.

"Don't take any more chew from the whiches," he said.

"I didn't."

"Twizzler?" said Kamil, looking at Nick.

Nick just stared back, then turned his chin to the TV.

"He's after you, Nick. You are the one, you are the difference, all the difference in the world.

"How you like it now?"

Nick did not acknowledge.

He let his eyes close, found the clicker thing on the bed frame, clicked it, and eased his schmucking head back.

CHAPTER THIRTY-THREE

"I know of no country in which there is so little independence of mind and real freedom of discussion as in America."

— *Alexis de Tocqueville*

Nick pushed the damn walker down the sidewalk, grumbling, lifting the god-damn thing up over every lip in the cement squares. He was hustling, not wanting to miss even warm-ups for the championship game.

He placed the walker, step, step, put down the damn walker, step, step, his cleats and glove swinging on the silver tubes.

"Schmuck this!" he roared as he threw the walker one-handed toward the sub-title bunker, landing, rolling and laying on the fine lawn like an unexploded grenade.

He threw his shoes over his shoulder.

"Oooh!"

He winced as one of the hard plastic cleats got him good in the back.

He put on his glove, pushed it into his face and sucked it down.

He drew it back a few inches to see the writing in the pocket. The glove had been his father's, and his grandfather's before him. Nick had never missed the celebrity softball tournament, but had never won.

This time he was winning.

He stopped on the sidewalk and held the glove, a "Babe Ruth Model B" in both hands, turning it this way, that, in and out of the sun, to see the old writing, in black pen, it seemed.

"To my son."

It was his grandfather's hand.

"Play catch with your son, even though I never played catch with you."

And then his own father's note.

He had copied the note above, misspelling "though."

Nick pressed the glove into his face, and then pulled it away, fearful he had already washed away the ink.

"Oh, brother," he said to himself.

He wiped his eyes with the back of his hand.

Nick straightened his back, did not watch his feet move except out the very, very bottom of his eyes, swung his arms at his side to imitate any normal person and felt his heart pound with each breath.

He smiled and waved, doffed his new cap to drivers, pointed at his jersey.

He wore the colors of The DeToqueville Mighty Ducks, jersey, pants, along with his new publishing boots.

Nick had only a few blocks to the park for the annual Celebrity History Softball Tournament to do battle with the Herodotus Flying Togas, The Toynbee Tigers, Thucydides All-Stars, the Durant-Durant Durants, and others. The Foucalt Foreign Legion had to drop out because too many of their players were out of town.

At the first hint of popcorn he cut across the big, rolling lawn.

Nick Green hobbled out of the grass, fleeing the mosquito posse, onto the tortuous sidewalk and the people.

Sun blotched the tree-lined walk.

Nick smiled at hearing the happy voices and having to dodge children running with abandon.

He made his way toward the field and slowed as the stream of people traffic made its way through the narrow gate.

He wore his glove and raised his chin, looking for his team.

He jumped a little when a dog licked his hand, then petted its head before it bolted off for new adventures.

Once inside the gate the flurry of activity intensified, like going round and round in a water park slide and hitting the bottom, whoosh!

Nick kept looking around, wearing his glove, lost like a child dropped off by his parents for his first day of T-ball.

And there they were, his people, his team, leaning on the fence behind home plate, watching the All-Stars and Flying Togas game, their fingers clutching the wire, just hoping for a foul ball to break their fingers.

That's the one thing Nick remembered about his father taking him to fast-pitch softball games right here, where he sat with all his friends right there in the first bench, behind home plate, grabbing Nick back and making a joke about how his stupid kid is going to get his fingers broke and he'll never play ball and turning around and having all those big men with their mouths wide open, laughing loud at him.

As he moved as fast as he could, dodging more dogs and kids, the blue, white and red, the French version of the uniforms, gave him a tingle.

This is where he belonged amid all this popcorn and hoopla, yellow mini-frisbees and blue cotton candy.

He put the glove to his face up to his eyebrows for a moment, then brought it down, quickly, as Lori Groome turned around and greeted him with a high-five and "there he is!" as if he were the one.

Nick saw the fingers of Lori Groome, Eddie, Principal Miss Bordeaux, Deanno, Honey White Bear-de la Rosa, stuck inside the fence, but he swallowed his admonitions.

He stood among them and watched the consolation game as Bobby Barkham, Hess Bangor, Fulton Crampton, Kamil K., Randy the reporter, Langley Harmsworth did battle with Daisy Doorknor, Doderic and Dora Nouwens, and the rest.

Nick looked around and saw Dollie Belle Lee-Thornpine in the stands wearing a big white sunhat, and the old man, in a tree, his bare feet dangling, his head down, whittling his pool cue, looking up just in time to see every pitch.

The crowd roared.

Not the crowd at the softball game, but somewhere else.

Nick looked to see.

He saw a bunch of people in a semi-circle around something, over by the horseshoe pit thing, past the horseshoe thing a ways.

"Sales Team Dunk Tank," said Honey, who had drifted over to stand next to him.

"Oh, yeah," said Nick.

Dora Nouwens tagged out Bobby Barkham at home plate in a cloud of dust that concealed both of them and the umpire for a few seconds before anyone could see the umpire making the out sign, thumbs straight up.

The Herodotus Flying Open Togas came a running and high-fiving and yelling, jumping up and down, bouncing.

The Thucydides All-Stars rushed the umpire, pushing against him, throwing their hands every way, screaming, making more dust, causing a commotion. Like a Peanuts panel cartoon, the scene moved stage right, all following Pigpen through the far gate.

The DeToqueville Mighty Ducks watched.

Once outside the gate, someone in the middle of the feisty dusty atom-packed-tight crowd screamed in agony, and the waiting Red And Gold ambulance back by the Port-au-Potties lazily started its sirens and lights and moseyed over, across the lawn, behind the grandstands.

"Okay, we're on," said Lori Groome.

Stone-faced, Eddie, Principal Miss Bordeaux, Deanno, Honey White Bear-de la Rosa and Nickostatos Green made their way through the little gate into the playing field area.

The DeToqueville Mighty Ducks began to occupy the third base dugout, spreading out their towels, duffel bags, gloves.

Deanno and Honey White Bear-de la Rosa climbed up to duct-tape the Ducks banner to the roof of the dugout.

Each went through their own very private pre-game ritual.

They began to apply their games faces, suntan lotion, eye black, body lotion. They hid pine tar in secret places on their uniforms. Principal Miss Bordeaux put her Chinese black op ninja death star in her sock.

Eddie patted the rosin bag all over his body.

Nick sat by himself at the end of the dugout bench, lacing up his shoes, glancing up with each eyelet to watch the Tigers warming up in front of the first base dugout.

A mascot wearing a tiger cub costume sat in the stands behind the first base dugout, methodically pounding a drum.

Boom-boom ... boom-boom ... boom-boom-boom.

Over and over.

Nick sensed the crowd growing.

Pickups full of people backed up to the outfield fence, Frisbees filled the air like gnats. The grandstands plugged in the open spaces.

One of the Tigers stuck a flag into the ground with a banner that said "Champions." The Tigers had not been beaten in the tournament for a long time.

The Toynbee Tigers lineup was unbeatable.

Captain Max Karp, Ph.D., World War I, World War II, University of Dayton, player-coach, held down third base like a concrete anchor.

Their lineup was murderer's row from leadoff to rover.

Bubba Carl Van Dyke, Ph.D. European History, University of Wisconsin

Molly Quizzinal, Ph.D. American History & Numismatics, University of Iowa

Julius Yoo, Ph.D., Ancient History, Texas A&M

Brule Becker, Ph.D., Dark Ages, University of Chicago

Florence Malmsbury, Ph.D., Classical Studies, Ohio State

Ambroise Hammad, Ph.D., The American West, American Folklore, Berkeley

Canoes and fishing boats and houseboats began to gather on the river to wait for their home runs.

Nick grabbed a softball from the ball bag and tossed it to Eddie. They began to warm up. Eddie swirled his left arm like a boat motor, then his right arm, then tossed the ball to Nick, who was already pissed.

Then it began.

"Ancient history," said Lori Groome, supposedly to her catch partner, Honey White Bear-de la Rosa, but loud enough for the Tigers to hear.

"Long enough," replied Honey.

"Goin' down," said Eddie.

"Goin' down hard," said Nick.

The crowd swarmed. The players moved around inside the hive humming around them.

Deanno nodded to Lori Groome and she threw the ball back to him, over his head, so he had to chase it over behind home plate.

"Tiger meat," whispered Deanno at Julius Yoo, the closest Tiger, as he picked up the errant throw.

Yoo swung around and stuck his chest into Deanno's face.

Deanno smooshed his nose into the letters on Yoo's green, yellow and white jersey. The teams ran over and a shoving, moving scrum formed behind home plate.

Fans climbed the fence behind home plate and screamed, shaking it.

"Get him!"

"Sock him!"

"Damn historians!"

"Stupid Ducks! Quaaack!"

The umpires, dressed in black, had just arrived, and they ran together to the fight.

"Hey, hey!" shouted Martha, who would have the plate.

"Break it up, break it up," said Mary, the base umpire for today's championship game.

"Hey, wait a minute!" said Nick, backing up, snatching his Yankees cap from the grass.

"Not those two."

He went right up to Martha, who was already sweeping the plate with a long broom.

"You can't be the umpires," said Nick.

"You are not neutral."

"Nothing you can do about it, sport. Play nice, now," she said, slamming her mask down over her face.

"Play ball!" she yelled.

The teams hustled back to their dugouts to get ready.

Harland Lombardi, the press box announcer, smoking a cigar, looked out an open window in the white wooden press box at the top of the grandstands along with Daisy Doorknor, his color commentator and spotter.

Fulton Crampton sat in the first row of the grandstand, still in his sweaty, dirty uniform, sharing his popcorn with The Big Boss From New York City, in his suit, but with the tie loosened, having flown in just this morning for this game.

Nick noticed as he was checking out the crowd and going over the Tiger lineup with his catcher Bambi Cartwright. He excused himself and climbed to the top of the dugout steps to get a better view.

He stared.

The guy with Fulton Crampton looked just very familiar.

Harland announced the lineups.

The players stood at attention along the first and third base lines as four fighter jets crashed the scene at tree-top level.

One of Katie's students, dressed as Lee Harvey Oswald, made her way to the microphone inside the pitcher's circle, holding the hand of one of Janey's children dressed as John Wilkes Booth. The two characters had their character names on masking tape on their backs, just to make sure.

The players removed their caps and held them at their chests as Oswald and Booth sang a national anthem duet.

Afterwards, Dollie Belle Lee-Thornpine threw out the first ball to catcher Cartwright of HR/PR.

Nick saw Crampton and The Big Boss eating out of the same large popcorn bag and remembered.

You weren't playin' ball, that's all. We're just here to clear up the misunderstanding.

INFORMATION IS Everything ... THE WHOLE BALLGAME ...

Nick took the gum out of his mouth and pulled from his back pocket the page he had torn from one of the sophomore history textbooks at the school.

He pushed the page into the gum with his palm on the cement block wall next to the lineup card.

History Is So Boring.

Teachers just go throo the motions. And then there was a drawing of a superhero firing laser beams or spider webs from its hands.

Pres'dents Book of Secrets

* * *

The honorary coaches, a giant Tony The Tiger for the Toynbee Tigers and Donald Duck for the DeToqueville Mighty Ducks, met at home plate with Martha and Mary in their black uniforms, Martha still wearing her mask.

The coaches exchanged lineup cards, faced off in classic boxer's pose for Randy the reporter on one knee in the grass behind home, and also Langley Harmsworth's photographer, shooting from his back.

Martha came around the plate and leaned low to dust it again, looking straight into the eyes of Bambi Cartwright, already in position.

"He who controls the past," said Martha.

"Controls the future," said Bambi.

"Just make him throw strikes," said Martha.

Martha spritely found her spot behind Bambi and pointed at Nick Green in the pitcher's circle as Harland Lombardi, relaying Daisy's whisper in his ear, announced the Tiger leadoff batter, shortstop Molly Quizzinal.

"Number 4," said Harland.

Martha continued to point, like Sakajawea, as Nick, his back to her, drew something in the dirt behind the circle.

"Play ball!" said Martha.

"What's she pointing at?" said Harland to Daisy.

Nick persisted with his foot figures.

When he had finished, he turned around, pounded the new ball into his glove and toed the rubber.

The little grey-haired old lady from the bakery walked down the first row of the grandstands making everyone look around her. She carried a dusty tray of Pre-History Cakes.

She stopped in front of The New York Big Boss.

Fulton Crampton caught the boss' eye and shook his head.

"Yeah, no, no thanks, thanks, though," The Big Boss said to the old lady.

She waited, holding the tray, staring The Big Boss in the eye, until Fulton Crampton hissed at her to "get the 'h' down the road."

She moved away slowly, staring at Fulton Crampton and The Big Boss.

"Mooolllyyy Quiii ... zz ... iii ... nal steps into the left-handed batter's box like she's been there before," said Harland Lombardi into the microphone.

"Nickostatos Greenberg in the blue, white and red uniform and blue and white and blue Yankees cap toes the rubber.

"Here's the pitch."

"Hey, hey!" some people turned around to stare at Harland Lombardi.

"This isn't radio, man. We can see. You just say some things, not every damn thing, c'mon, man, haven't you been to a ballgame before?"

And then some people turned around and said, "Hey, let him, go ahead. It's something different at least."

Harland Lombardi looked at Daisy to see what she thought.

She smiled to say, keep talking.

Harland Lombardi described the *high, wonderful, rainbow-like arc* of Nick's first pitch.

It landed in Bambi's upturned glove, just behind home plate.

"Ball one," said Martha, nonplussed.

"What?" Bambi turned around to say.

"What!" said Nick.

Nick shook his head and turned away to pick up the resin bag and fire it at the ground as Harland described every action and emotion of Nick, Bambi, Martha and Molly.

Harland put his hand over the mic to ask Daisy if she could read what Nick had written in the infield dirt behind the pitcher's circle. It was upside down, facing toward the outfield.

She shrugged, folded a napkin and dropped it into the box next to her.

Quizzinal grounded out to Mighty Duck shortstop Kolya Zuyev, manager of wood products, for out number one in a boom-boom play at first.

Nick got Hammad on a come-backer and Malmsbury popped out to first for an easy top of the first.

Bringing the Ducks to bat.

"Kathryn 'Bambi' Cartwright," catcher, batting lead-off for the Mighty Ducks," announced Harland Lombardi.

Bambi looked back and flapped a quick wave to Harland.

"Hi," he said over the loudspeaker.

Harland felt the heat of Daisy's eyes on his cheek.

"Cartwright grounds out ... *weakly* ... to Ambroise Hammad, Ph.D., The American West, American Folklore, Berkeley, second baseman for the Toynbee Tigers in their home white, yellow and green.

Bambi Cartwright touched first base, then took the long way back to the third base dugout, by way of the middle of the infield, almost touching second base, to read what Nick had written.

"Whatever it is," said Harland into the loudspeakers atop the press box and attached to nine light poles around the field, also being transmitted via WHOKNEW radio to five thousand homes in the county, "it touched her heart. Just look at the new look of determination on the face of Kathryn 'Bambi' Cartwright in the blonde plait dangling down her back almost to her waist."

The second out went by without Harland Lombardi really noticing as he folded about ten napkins in a row.

"The Ducks go down quietly," said Harland after the third out was recorded on a line drive to third sacker Karp.

On their way into the dugout, each of the Tigers made sure to go read what Nick had written with his right foot from left to right in the dirt behind the pitcher's circle. Not one of them tried to disturb it. They walked respectfully around the writing and made eye contact with a Duck, nodding.

"It's on," said Eddie to Honey White Bear-de la Rosa as they each grabbed their gloves to take the field.

"What is on?" said Honey White Bear-de la Rosa.

"I do not know," said Eddie.

"But it is."

"You got that right," said Honey.

They each paused at the writing, then high-fived each other with their gloves and pointed at the Tiger dugout, then sprinted to their posts.

The players and fans stopped what they were doing to look up at a small plane pulling a banner promoting the upcoming Sub-Title Banquet and The BIG Pageant. They reached up to catch one of the thousands of plastic packets of moist towlettes announcing the upcoming "Freedom Dog" eating contest that night.

Behind the stands a volunteer band played the fife and a drum.

Someone shot fireworks into the sky from the back of a pickup on the other side of the centerfield fence.

The smell of powder drifted in with the northerly breeze.

With the beverage hawkers having had a chance by now to get around to the outfield, the pickets of the Mighty Ducks and Tigers began to yell at each other from the left and right field fence lines.

The ceremonial coaches, gigantic Donald Duck and Tony The Tiger, paced back and forth in front of their dugouts as the fireworks continued and the haze fogged the field. They pointed and shouted instructions that no one could hear or understand or was interested in. They continued to shout and point and pace and worry.

Nick, sensing this was his moment, stepped back from the rubber, causing Martha to straighten behind Bambi, and Bambi to remove her mask.

The batter, Bubba Carl Van Dyke, Ph.D. European History, University of Wisconsin, put one foot out of the batter's box and turned to Martha, asking for time.

Nick began to mumble something, an incantation, a prayer, a verse, an epithet.

"Hey, batter, batter ..."

"What's he saying?" said Harland to Daisy and everyone heard.

Nick continued, holding his glove to his chest and peering out over the top.

"Nick Green, Duck hurler and 3B 1K general manager has gone insane," said Harland. "No just kidding. What? I was kidding."

"Heeeyy, batta-batta," Nick hummed.

"The pageant will be different."

"The books will be different. They will be on time. The sales team will make sales. The company will go on. We will ignore the big boss, because I don't believe he is the big boss, anyway.

"Hey, batta-batta. Hey!"

People in the grandstands turned around to Harland in the press box.

"What's he saying?"

Nick stepped to the unattached orange rubber, seeming to have come out of a trance.

He twirled his right arm as he did with every soft toss, trying to confuse the batter as to when he would release it.

"Hey, batter, batter!" he said.

"Hey! *Shoe's* untied."

And there came the uphill-downhill pitch, designed to rise up high and come down in such a way as to be difficult to hit squarely.

"And there it goes," said Harland Lombardi, describing how Bubba Carl Van Dyke, formerly of Wisconsin, hit the new white ball a ton, and how now the boaters were paddling and diving and crashing like factory trout after a hunk of white bread.

The giant Duck and Tiger paced, wearing paths in the good grass. More pickups with fireworks joined the fray. Smoke and the stench of sweat and smoke choked the air. The right field fans put together a rhyme that completely spelled out and dishonored the lives of the left field crowd and were then completely taken aback when the left fielders replied in kind and better.

White and red grape shot, left over from the cafeteria battlefield, were lobbed over the fence by some of the sweaty members of Union #374, exploding right inside the Tiger dugout, spraying, causing subs and regulars to dive for cover where it could be found.

The game wore on, 1-0, until the Mighty Ducks broke through the Tiger line, scoring two runs on a Honey White Bear-de la Rosa intentional walk since Brule Becker was her freshman year sweetheart, a sacrifice bunt by Nickostatos Greenberg, putting White Bear-de la Rosa on second with one out.

Buddy Fowler, maintenance and landscaping, grounded to Malmsbury at second. She bobbled it, placing White Bear-de la Rosa on third and Fowler on first, still with just one out.

Deanno came to the plate.

He hit Becker's second pitch, a secret-weapon whistler, right back to the mound. Becker fired it to Yoo, his catcher, who screamed back at him that it was not a force play.

"No force! No force!"

Bases loaded.

John Brown, focus groups, margins and spacing, paper thickness, rover, strode to the plate, making a line in the sand as he dragged his big aluminum bat.

He smacked a frozen rope to center field, scoring White Bear-de la Rosa and Fowler, pulling the Big Ducks into the lead, 2-1.

And that's the way it stayed ... until the penultimate inning, the top of the sixth.

Seeing the scene from his vantage, realizing what was happening, Harland Lombardi's heart pounded.

His eyes teared. He gripped the microphone and tried to remain calm even in the face of all that was right in front of him.

He must record this, he told himself, for who would ever be able to imagine.

His voice became deep and un-accented.

Daisy wiped the sweat from his brow and his nose with one of her precious napkins.

"We should play softball only, only when it is worthwhile going to certain death, as now," said Harland Lombardi.

"Then there would not be softball because Florence Malmsbury had offended Eddie.

"And when there was a softball game, like this one, it would be softball! And then the determination of the teams would be quite different. Then all these whom The Big Duck is leading would not follow him into Russia, and we should not go to fight in Austria and Prussia without knowing why."

Those casually listening at home fell to their knees in front of the radio.

"Softball is not courtesy but the most horrible thing in life; and we ought to understand that and not play at slow-pitch. We ought to accept this terrible necessity sternly and seriously. It all lies in that: get rid of falsehood and let softball be war and not a game. As it is now, slow-pitch is the favorite pastime of the idle and frivolous. The celebrity team history week calling is the most highly honored."

Nick raised his hand and formed a fist and shouted.

All the Mighty Ducks in the field said, "Hurrah!" and bent low to get into good fielding position, while those on the Duck bench rushed to the little fence in front of the dugout and climbed it, raising their fists, shouting, their faces red and the veins in their necks bulging pretty big.

"But what is softball? What is needed for success in slow-pitch? What are the habits of the players? The aim of softball is murder; the methods of slow-pitch are spying, treachery, and their encouragement, the ruin of a country's inhabitants, robbing them or stealing to provision the army, and fraud and falsehood termed ballplayer craft."

Brule Beck, Ph.D., Dark Ages, University of Chicago, hit a gapper, rounded first and dived headfirst into second base.

"The habits of the player class are the absence of freedom, that is, discipline, idleness, ignorance, cruelty, debauchery, and drunkenness. And in spite of all this it is the highest class, respected by everyone. All the kings, except the Chinese, wear softball uniforms, and he who scores the most runs receives the highest rewards."

Duck second baseman Eddie took the relay from shortstop Principal Miss Bordeaux, and put his knee down to block the bag as he applied the tag.

Able, Janey's son, heard it all from the northeast corner of the Duck cement block dugout, hands over his ears, knees pulled to his chest. He was thinking of the inevitable time when he would be called to pinch-hit or pinch run, and would he be able to actually do it, when the time came.

"They meet to defeat one another; they strike out and throw out tens of thousands, and then have thanksgiving services for having struck out so many people (they even exaggerate the number), and they announce a victory, supposing that the more people they have struck out the greater their achievement."

Harland Lombardi's chest heaved. Daisy wiped his brow. His lip quivered. He gripped the microphone stand thing tight in both hands.

Becker's right hand and left hand ran full force into Eddie's left thigh, bending every one, breaking some, gashing Eddie's thigh.

Able looked at the men and women around him in the dugout. He saw their eyes and their mouths wide open, in ecstasy or agony, he could not tell. Sounds leaked into his ears and he pressed his hands tighter.

"How does God above look at them and hear them?" exclaimed Harland Lombardi in a shrill, piercing voice.

Blood stained Eddie's pants and the dust and the bag, and the ball. They both lay on the ground, unable to move. The ambulance lights and sirens lazily revved up and the ambulance ambled over the lawn, later explaining that they could not go any faster because someone forgot to take care of the lawn and it was full of bumpy nightcrawler holes.

Stretcher carriers finally waddled out to the second base area.

"Ah, my friend, it has of late become hard for me to live."

Harland Lombardi put one arm around Daisy Doorknor and pulled her close.

"I see that I have begun to understand too much. And it doesn't do for man to taste of the tree of knowledge of good and evil ...

"Ah, well, it's not for long!" he added.

Nick leaped into the air and pumped his fist as Max Karp swung at the third strike and missed.

Falling on both knees, Karp put his head to the dirt and pounded his fist. He roared into the dirt, filling his mouth with dust.

Which he regretted almost right away.

CHAPTER THIRTY-FOUR

"Time is but the stream I go a-fishing in."
— *Henry David Thoreau*

Harland Lombardi saw Randy the reporter and Langley Harmsworth sitting in the stands just below the press box. He caught Randy's eye and waved them up.

Daisy scooched over to make room for Randy and Langley Harmsworth, pushing her napkin cardboard box under the table.

They opened the other window so everyone got the fresh air, watching the between-innings activities.

"Pretty good game, huh?" said Harland Lombardi.

"Yeah," said Randy.

Langley Harmsworth nodded.

They watched Martha take off her mask and head out to the middle of the infield to confer with Mary. They stood behind whatever it was that Nick had written.

"What does that say?" said Harland.

"It's upside down, whatever it is," said Randy.

Langley Harmsworth nodded, fitting popcorn into her mouth one kernel at a time.

"They say the game has to be in the bag, no chances," said Mary to Martha.

Mary held her black umpire's hat to her mouth to speak.

Martha showed her back to the grandstands, though the people behind the straight-away center field fence could read her lips if they really tried.

None did.

"How do you know?" said Martha.

Mary put the hat in her mouth and made hieroglyphics with her hands, cave drawings.

Martha looked back over her shoulder and saw Fulton Crampton making similar signs with his hands, using a popcorn bag as a prop or indicator or decoy.

She turned back to Mary.

"D'ya think we even need to, Mar?"

Mary nodded at Nick's cursive footwriting.

"Yeah," said Martha, "maybe you're right."

With authority she pulled her mask on and pivoted to return to her post.

Nick toed the movable orange rubber after finishing his warm-up tosses, waiting for a batter.

Everyone looked impatiently toward the Toynbee Tiger dugout. They had shit to do after this.

The New York City Big Boss leaned to Fulton Crampton.

"You tell the bitch, I mean, you know. It's in the bag, right?"

Fulton Crampton nodded, totally unsure.

The Toynbee Tony The Tiger strode resolutely to the home plate area, dragging the biggest bat in the Tiger bat rack, kicking up dust.

Martha took off her mask and smiled, expecting this was another gag routine she had to act like she just enjoyed the crap out of.

Langley elbowed Randy in the side.

"Geez," he scowled at her and people in the stands looked up at the press box.

Langley Harmsworth nodded at the field.

"Oh," said Randy. "Why dintya just say?

"Umm, Harland, there's something we prob'ly want to add right now."

"Yes," said Harland, "go right ahead, Randy the reporter, the floor is yours, as it was."

"Well," said Randy.

"In that article, ya know, about the death of Blaze Thornpine, and all, the one that got the press award that's in the front window at the paper?"

"Yep," said Harland. "Haven't seen it yet, heard a lot of good things about it."

"Well, hmmm, how do I?"

The Big Tiger, with the big feet and long tail, big paws, big Tiger head, dragged the long, thick aluminum-alloy bat behind Martha, not acting like it wanted to talk to her at all.

It stopped and took a few practice swings.

The crowd laughed a little.

Nick stared and tossed the ball in one hand.

The Mighty Duck mascot coach made a scene over in front of the third base dugout, raising its hand, putting its hand on its head, kneeling and putting its big head in its big yellow duck hands.

The Tiger rested the bat on the ground, between its legs and began to remove the big Tiger head.

Langley Harmsworth elbowed Randy again, harder.

"Umm," he said.

"There's something we did not exactly include."

"Oh, yeah?" said Harland, looking over at Randy, smiling, enjoying the Tiger skit.

The head came off and the crowd roared. Some people ran, others moved to another spot just to be moving. And then everything was quiet.

The Mighty Duck mascot coach knelt in the grass.

As Randy said over the loudspeakers and into the homes what everyone at the ballpark already knew.

"Umm, yeah.

"Umm, Blaze Thornpine ain't exactly dead."

CHAPTER THIRTY-FIVE

"If a man insisted always on being serious, and never allowed himself a bit of fun and relaxation, he would go mad or become unstable without knowing it."
— Schmucking Herodotus

"What the?" said Nick.

"Yeah, what the?" said Harland over the loudspeakers and into the homes to Randy the reporter.

"Well, umm," said Randy.

He put his arm down to block another elbow by Langley Harmsworth, but *did* notice her nod, that she was nodding at Fulton Crampton and The New York City Big Boss turning around.

Randy the reporter, as everyone knew him, looked right into Fulton Crampton's wide eyes that sought to remind him succinctly how and why his wife had died.

"An actor ... did not die," said Randy over the loudspeaker.

The headless Tiger, Blaze Thornpine, tossed the lifeless head aside, picked up the bat and stepped into the box. He tapped the plate while eyeing Nick Green.

"Huh?" said Harland, grabbing the mic back.

Randy took the mic from Harland and leaned it way over on the edge of its base, toward himself.

"Supposed to provoke antipathy towards Nick. That's what they said."

"Ant ... path ... y?" said Harland, again grabbing the mic out of Randy's hand and leaning it back on its base more over toward him.

"Antipathy," said Randy, shouting.

"What is anti-pathy?" said Harland.

"Yeah!" yelled the crowd and the people on their knees at home.

"What is it!"

Martha leaned low over Bambi Cartwright's inside shoulder, ready to call the first pitch to Blaze Thornpine, as Harland received some notes from Daisy.

"Now ... now, now," said Harland Lombardi, the microphone now echoing for some reason.

"Pinch, pinch, pinch hitting for the Toynbee Tigers, umm, ummm, um, Blaze Thooorrrnpiiine, West Liberty University, West Liberty, West Virginia, Roman Empire, Civil War.

Martha watched Blaze digging in, the serious look on his face.

"This is slow-pitch softball son, not the Battle of Bull Run. You're wearin' half a tiger costume, your adversary is a giant duck. Don't wet yourself," she said.

"Anti-pathy?" said Harland.

"Why so? How so? May I ask?"

"It would just make it seem like he wasn't able to handle things and they knew he wanted to change the history books all along, and they weren't going to let him," said Randy as they fought over control of the microphone stand thing.

"They?" said Harland.

"They who?"

Langley Harmsworth nodded and Randy pointed out of the press box down to where Fulton Crampton and The New York City Big Boss had been sitting, but now, since the old lady with the old cakes had been watching them closely, she had grabbed the empty space.

Nick, listening to the game report coming from the press box, looked at Blaze Thornpine, at where Fulton Crampton and The New York City Big Boss used to be, and then pointed to his own dugout.

He walked toward the third baseline, tossing the big white ball in one hand like an upside-down yo-yo, staring through the screen of the little fence that protected the dugout, into the far corner.

He stopped just short of the foul line and pointed again, kept pointing, like ol' Babe Ruth toward center field.

Langley Harmsworth nodded, so subtly, but Randy noticed, and so did Harland Lombardo and Daisy Doorknob.

Able appeared out the far end of the Mighty Ducks cement block dugout. As in a dream he walked toward Nick as Nick tossed the ball, up, down.

The old man sitting in the tree behind the Ducks dugout all of a sudden hopped to stand on the branch, drew the pool cue back into an expert authentic, classic tribesman pose, and hurled the pool cue, over the backstop fence in a perfect arc, popping right into the small of Hess Bangor's back as he lay stretched out atop the press box roof, his head hanging down, trying to see into the open press box window.

"Oooof!" Hess Bangor ooofed into the microphone and over the crowd.

He reached way back and rubbed his back and continued to lay on the press box roof and lean down toward the open press box window.

Out of the shadows of the trees behind the grandstands, where they had been resting like lions since after the sales team dunk tank had shut down so everyone could go watch the game, one by one, came The Generals: Artie, Eddie, Jose, Willie, Roy, Juanita, Fred, Clarence, Earl, Manuel, Rita, Ray, Marvin, Floyd.

Kamil K., sitting low behind the giant white steering wheel in his faded lime-green Pontiac in a spot that only he knew about, where you could sit in your car and watch the game and honk your horn, honked his horn.

All around the field horns began honking like geese wanting butter on these damn bread crumbs.

People at home got off their knees, ran outside and honked their car horns.

Blaze Thornpine, still bent over, watched as Able snagged the ball in mid-air and headed toward the pitcher's circle.

Martha held her mask at her side as she visited with Bambi Cartwright. Able tossed the ball in one hand as he made his way to the unattached orange rubber lying cockeyed in the middle of the infield.

CHAPTER THIRTY-SIX

"Time is the fairest and toughest judge."

— *Edgar Quinet*

"He doesn't have a glove."

Daisy whispered into Harland's ear as Langley Harmsworth nodded at Able on the mound, toeing the rubber, tossing the big white ball, up, down.

Blaze Thornpine took his stance in the batter's box and Martha slammed her mask down again, groaned and leaned low over Bambi Cartwright's inside shoulder.

Nick's teammates gathered around him in the dugout and asked why he didn't want to pitch to Blaze Thornpine.

"I couldn't get him out," said Nick.

"It was time for someone else to give it a try."

"But you didn't even try!"

"Not this time," said Nick.

"But last year and the year before that, remember?"

"Oh, yeah," someone said.

"Oh, yeah."

"And I want to ..." said Nick as he sat to change shoes.

CHAPTER THIRTY-SEVEN

"He put in your heart certain wishes and plans; in my heart he put other different desires."

— Sitting Bull

Able pulled his arm back slowly, and unlike Nick's high, gentle arc, he fired an underhand toss right into the strike zone.

Blaze Thornpine, surprised, was able to get his bat on the ball and launch it toward the bleachers along the right field foul line.

John Brown, Mighty Ducks right fielder, headed for the ball, the fence and the crowd.

He reached up just as he was about to catch up to the ball, gouging his stomach into the fence and vaulting himself over the fence and into the stands, crashing people, popcorn and poplar.

Once in the stands John Brown shared a death grip on the big white ball with one of the fans. They gritted their teeth, their faces turned red and their neck veins bulged.

All was relayed over the loudspeaker and radio by Harland Lombardi and color commentator Randy the reporter while Hess Bangor leaned low, just his eyes showing beneath the window frame, his stringy hair giving away his position to anyone interested.

The fan, keeping one hand on the large ball, grabbed John Brown around the throat with his other hand, and so John Brown did the same.

The Giant Duck continued to pace, put its hands on its head, over its face, throw its arms all about, opened its mouth though no noise emitted, while the battle raged in the right field bleachers.

For some seconds they gazed with frightened eyes at one another's unfamiliar faces and both were perplexed at what they had done and what they were to do next. "Am I taken prisoner or have I taken him prisoner?" each was thinking.

But the French officer was evidently more inclined to think he had been taken prisoner because Pierre's strong hand, impelled by instinctive fear, squeezed his throat ever tighter and tighter.

The Frenchman was about to say something, when just above their heads, terrible and low, a cannon ball whistled, and it seemed to Pierre that the French officer's head had been torn off, so swiftly had he ducked it.

Both John Brown and the fan were startled when the next ball banged into the stands.

They looked together as Martha, Bambi Cartwright, Blaze Thornpine and Able each stared at them with their arms wide and up around their shoulders to indicate, "Hey, let's go! Geez."

As the fan climbed under the bleachers to retrieve the big white ball, John Brown hopped the fence to return to his post just as Blaze Thornpine grounded out weakly to second and the sales team — Antoinette, Cid, Stan, and Jean, all wearing soaked T-shirts and shorts and tennis shoes arrived at the game after having drained the dunk tank and put everything away.

Langley Harmsworth's photographer balanced on one foot in front of them in the third base bleachers and began taking photos.

Meanwhile, Austin Bellincioni, the accountant, walked over to them with his hand out to count the money they had made.

The Mighty Duck dugout chanted, "one down, two to go, one down, two to go."

Able got the next two batters on a pop up to short center field and a dribbler back to the mound.

The Mighty Ducks threw their gloves into the air, stormed the pitchers circle and fell into a pile.

The Toynbee Tigers waited for the nonsense to end, and then formed a line.

The two teams shook hands and then stood together to read what what Nick had written:

"Histry is writtn by the winners." — Donald Duck

"Okay," said Max Karp, nodding and patting Able on the back.

"Okay," said Able.

Harland Lombardi mumbled into the microphone.

"I wonder what it says?"

Daisy shook her head and crawled to the floor to retrieve her box.

Harland watched Randy and Langley Harmsworth on the field talking to the players.

CHAPTER THIRTY-EIGHT

"Well, first, I didn't kill Dr. King."

— *James Earl Ray*

By this time Nick had forgotten about his heart, about the game, about the history book, and about Pre-History cakes.

He wanted to find Fulton Crampton and The Big NYC Boss and find out WTF about Blaze Thornpine?

He fast-hobbled over the big lawn to the long sidewalk, headed back to the office. Maybe they would go there and just try to take over.

He stopped and watched as the shuttle bus putted past with Fulton Crampton and The Big NYC Boss Man sitting in the back, holding on with one hand, their feet dangling.

They watched each other and did not wave as the airport shuttle rattled off, down the street, into the sunset.

CHAPTER THIRTY-NINE

"Boy, I love talking about the Kennedy assassination, man. That's my favorite topic. You know why? Because to me it's a great example of, er, a totalitarian government's ability to, you know, manage information and thus keep us in the dark any way they ... Oh, sorry. Wrong meeting ... Ah, schmuck. That's the meeting we're having tomorrow at the docks.

"I love talking about Kennedy. I was just down in Dallas, Texas. You know you can go down there and, ah, to Dealey Plaza where Kennedy was assassinated. And you can actually go to the sixth floor of the School Book Depository. It's a museum called ... The Assassination Museum. I think they named that after the assassination. I can't be too sure of the chronology here, but ...

"Anyway they have the window set up to look exactly like it did on that day. And it's really accurate, you know. 'Cause Oswald's not in it."

— Bill Hicks

"They had been found out about Blaze Thornpine, wanted to leave. You won't see them again. Not for a while."

Nick sat in the waiting area of the main office talking to Joan McCarthy, who was actually Daisy's boss. He'd almost forgot, but had been on maternity leave, and now, since Daisy was going to marry Harland Lombardi and maybe do something, it seemed like a perfect time for

Joan McCarthy to come back to work.

"You know, right?" she said.

"Why did B.T. appear there, then," said Nick.

"Where had he been? Who knew about it? What did his wife know? Where is he now? Nobody has seen him since the game."

"People will debate that for years, Nick. Meanwhile, life goes on, huh?" said Joan McCarthy as she took a call.

She put up a finger and Nick gulped his question about who burned down the castle and who fake-killed Blaze Thornpine in the first place.

Joan McCarthy folded her hands on her desk and smiled in the direction of the front door. Nick followed her eyes to the delegation of The Gluers & Historians Combined Union #375 now filling the foyer fairly fast.

"That sounds good, real good," Nick said as he shook Max Karp's hand and then Norsy Doorknor. He patted backs and walked with the delegation to the front door.

He took a deep breath, pivoted on one foot and turned to smile at Joan McCarthy and saw Daisy sitting in her place.

"Well, hello, Miss Daisy, how are you? What happened to Joan?"

"Knocked up," said Daisy.

"Oh," said Nick. "Again, huh?"

"Yep," said Daisy.

Well, and so, things were kind of happening fast again around the book publishing plant.

They kind of had to.

They only had days to get ready for the banquet and the pageant and then the release of the book, and sending it out the goddamned door.

The sales teams drove all around town, worked the phones all around the country, drove all around the county and pretty near just drove each other crazy, day and night.

The new gluers and historians union had agreed to disagree about what exists and what is history in order to kind of keep their lifestyle as they had become accustomed to going smoothly and such.

The historians agreed to read some things online that Nick said Daisy wanted to show them.

Nick rode the riding lawn mower around the big lawn as the regular guy had gone fishing again, and it gave him a chance to think, and he thought that things were kind of going great at the moment, everyone kind of working toward a common goal, in a way.

It seemed like every hour Daisy ran out to him with a paper in her hand announcing some sort of progress had been made.

Margins ... done!

Spacing ... done!

Fonts ... done!

Spacing ... done right!

Paper ... figured out ... done!

Nick kept an eye toward the sub-title bunker and finally, there it was, white smoke poured from the stack connected to the underground.

They had a sub-title.

Woo-hoo!

Nick rocked east and west, mowing the fairway on No. 6 when ... there came Daisy sprinting like a character on Little House, and you just know she's going to fall. And she does. And she got up, and kept going.

And you just go, *aaaah.*

Out of breath but still able to smile wide with her eyes, she handed him the note that said they had cover art, completed, front and back.

And then they waited.

One day, two days.

At noon of the third day, and the text of the new book was not even yet a rumor, Nick sat on the front steps of his home, picking at his teeth with a toothpick, bouncing a fishing pole between his knees.

He waved at his son and daughter coming up the walk from the plant.

They waved back, walking slow, dejectedly.

"What's a matter?" he said.

"It's not going well," said Nick's son.

"They need help," said his daughter. "They can't think outside the box."

"Or take it to the next level," said the boy, not so young anymore.

"Dad, at the end of the day," said the girl, also getting up there. "They're all on the same page.

"That's not a good thing."

"Well," said Nick, whipping the pole in a fake practice cast.

"What can we do?"

Just then, explosions roared from where the son and daughter of Nickostatos Greenberg had just come.

Horses whinnied, a cannon shot.

Nick thought he saw a clump of dirt high in the air.

"Must be that Civil War reenactment," he said.

"They're not supposed to do that until the fall, after golf league."

The boy and girl sat on the steps.

"Hey," said Nick.

"Where do you guys work? I haven't seen you."

The boy shook his head.

"Doesn't matter," said the girl.

"We have something to tell you."

Nick flicked the pole again.

"There is something happening at the plant," said the girl.

"It's not good," the boy quickly got his part in.

"Yes," the girl turned toward Nick, getting excited.

"There are Roman Legions, on horseback."

"And chariots," said the boy, wagging his head.

"Really?" said Nick.

"Really?"

He grabbed the railing to pull himself up and tried to look.

The girl and boy grabbed him gently to push him back down.

"Really? Now this?" said Nick, setting the fishing pole aside, firing the toothpick at the lawn.

"And aliens," said the girl, looking right into her father's eyes.

"Spears piercing stomachs and arses."

"Are you kidding me? Are you schmucking kidding me? Aliens. Oh, God, aliens," said Nick. "And arses?"

"Vikings," she said.

"Oh, God, Vikings."

"Goths," said the boy.

"Visigoths. Huns," said the girl.

"Visihuns," said the boy.

"Visihuns! Omygod, I give up. I just give up!

"I can't do this," said Nick.

He stood atop the porch, hands on hips, staring in the direction of the plant, imagining all that was going on, and even if he went there and got everything in order, how could he get the new book back on track again, and then there's Daisy's wedding coming up, and The Sub-Title Banquet, those triangle sandwiches, Honey White Bear and those damn floats, got to be all changed, she's going to love that.

"We know Dad."

The young girl, now already a head taller than Nick, stood on the second step and looked into his eyes, placed a hand gently on his shoulder.

"We know, Father.

"We sort of already took over. You weren't looking. We got some of our best minds on this. I think you'll be pleased. It's actually going fine."

"Yeah," said the boy. "You can chill.

"We were just kidding like there was a big war there. We just been thinking about history all night, doing history things. You know how it goes."

"No Visihuns?" said Nick.

"No Visihuns, not one," said the girl.

"No, I don't really," said Nick.

"I was never much of a writer. Mowing the lawn is actually probably my favorite thing."

"And fishing?" said the girl, nodding toward the pole lying on the porch.

The boy balanced on the railing, walking up toward them, arms straight out.

"Careful, you'll," said Nick, reaching, then pulling his hand back as the boy made it safely to the top.

"Well, fishing, yeah, but I never, you know."

"We'd like to go fishing," said the boy.

"Not today," said the girl.

"You should come with us."

She took Nick by the elbow.

They walked with Nick, arm in arm, down their walk, through the gate, then down the middle of the street.

Nick looked back and saw his wife and more children following.

They crossed main street and entered the plant campus area, across lawns, through an opening in the hedge, onto the grass of the big lawn, past the sub-title bunker fence, they walked arm in arm.

They entered the front door of The New History Castle, down the marble steps to the basement, which had not been damaged in The Big History Castle Fire Of A Few Months Ago.

"Close your eyes," said Nick's daughter, still holding him under one arm.

They made it to the bottom of the marble staircase and Nick could feel they were entering a big space.

He thought to make a comment about how it was cooler down here and did not.

"Okay, open 'em," said the girl to her father.

Nick opened his eyes and saw The Big Room, as it was called in certain circles.

He looked about and saw the historians seated at the big tables with big books and big notebooks and computers and cords spread out covering the big tables.

Seated with the historians were children, young people, elementary school, middle school, junior high, high school, conferring with the historians, writing on notebooks, punching the keyboards.

The room buzzed with talk and excitement.

On the big screen a projector placed the full color image of the new front cover.

And on the side walls two other projectors placed the room-sized images of the new back cover of the Sophomore History 101 textbook.

"You always wanted us to take over," said the daughter.

"When you were in the hospital," she said.

"Well, it was just seeming to be getting to you. We want you to be around for a long, long time."

"And a book is just a book, said the wife, coming up to hug him, along with all the rest of their children.

"It is just paper and cardboard, some ink, some white space. You are flesh and blood," she said, hugging him around the waist.

"You are history."

They hugged and walked on over to the big tables and visited with Janey and Katie who were working along with their students.

Able sat with them, on his knees on a chair, directing a conversation on a project on a particular chapter, wearing a white T-shirt, just as everyone else in the room, with an image of Eddie's drawing of the superhero firing laser beams from its hands, and Eddie's note that had been in all of the previous sophomore history texts.

CHAPTER FORTY

"I have written too much history to have faith in it; and if anyone thinks I'm wrong, I am inclined to agree with him."
— Henry Adams

Through the night and on noon of the next day word came from The Big Room that by the next morning they should be pretty close.

Sitting with his back to his desk, his feet on the window sill, Nick groaned in despair, "pretty close?"

Even though the messenger had left the room and only Hess Bangor leaning on the door was listening, Nick said to the window, "Honey needs those chapters yesterday and she is going to be so angry.

"Even if she doesn't quit or put the whole town against us, the pageant will never be ready on time, the books won't get the proper launch, the sales teams won't be able to bring their clients in to the sub-title banquet to close and then the pageant and we won't sell any books and we will lose the contracts, all our money and The Big Boss will buy us anyway and he'll make history whatever he wants, and the world will burn."

"They already own you, if you believe what they said," said Hess Bangor as he locked his office door and turned to leave, carrying a black briefcase.

"I do and I don't," said Nick.

He pushed off the sill, spun around and saw Hess' back and hurrying in was Eddie with a piece of paper in his hand.

He stopped at the doorway and read from the paper, torn from something, a notebook, a book.

"Make up some shit," said Eddie.

He looked up to see if Nick was listening.

"Why not? Think out of the box. Don't be confined to what others say the world must be like."

Nick could see that Eddie clearly had not written what he was reading.

"Right? Take it to the next level. And stay on the same page. Be all you can be. I know, right?"

"Thanks, Eddie," said Nick, kicking off from his desk, twirling around, and smacking the bull moose head above him with a Cheetos cheese curl that he meant to toss into its mouth.

"You're a good man."

Nick said to Eddie.

Hess Bangor.

The Moose.

Or to himself.

CHAPTER **FORTY-ONE**

"Education is learning what you didn't even know you didn't know."

— *Daniel J. Boorstin*

As tradition goes, by this time after so much Capitalizing of Events and Traditions, and with all the energy being put into the still to come Sub-Title Banquet and The Pageant, the rolling off the presses of the first new book consisted only of Nick Green waiting at the bottom of a metal chute marked "Books" in black Magic Marker.

He flipped through the heavy thing, turned it over to see the back cover and hustled it over to Eddie for his John Hancock imprimatur.

Eddie took the book to the bathroom to sit with it for a while, came out smiling and handed it back to Nick.

They were almost there, thought Nick, when all the books would come tumbling down the chute, packed onto pallets, shrink-wrapped, hustled by forklifts onto the stout little delivery trucks all ready with their brand new cheerful lettering and design.

But first came the detestable ceremony and tradition of the taking of the new chapters to Honey White Bear-de la Rosa and The Daughters Of The So Last Century.

At Honey's recommendation, the loudspeakers around town played "Teach Your Children."

"Well?" everyone who heard it said the word softly to themselves.

It also played on the radio, over and over.

Nick carried the first new book out of his office, past Daisy's desk, surrounded by boxes of folded napkins, out the front door and the lawn and the little hole in the hedge to the big long sidewalk toward downtown, then turning to cross the street, march uphill to the school.

Halfway up the hill he got a ride from Kamil K.

There was nowhere to park so Kamil let Nick out in front and cruised around the block to look for an open spot.

Nick jogged across the street, right in front of someone, then to the school auditorium with The Daughters Of The Last Century in their period costumes sweating and waiting on the stage.

Wanting to get it over, Nick Green marched right in and up the middle aisle, through a clutter of janitors leaning on brooms and sweeping at nothing because people expected to see them working.

The waiting high school band didn't see him until he was halfway up and then scrambled to get everyone going and by the time he reached the stage, they clunked out the first notes of the big entrance song.

Honey White Bear-de la Rosa let him stand down there holding out the book for someone to take it.

She slowly approached the microphone, gave her prepared statement, welcoming everyone to this monstrous occasion.

"For our town, our region, our world," she said.

She nodded at the ceremonial steps leading to the stage.

Nick walked over, put one foot on the steps and reached up with both hands to Honey.

"Here," he said.

Honey smiled and hissed something under her breath.

She held the new sophomore history text up over her head for all to see and everyone applauded, lightly.

She looked at the front and back cover, flipped the pages, and as tradition had it, she would then pronounce the book worthy, hold it again high and everyone would applaud a little louder, then everyone could go home.

Rather, Honey White Bear-de la Rosa turned and called The Daughters over. They rose from their metal folding chairs, holding up their long dresses, and all came together in a very fluffy, starched circle, with hats also competing for precious air space.

The high school band, seated behind The Daughters, continued to play their special Neil Diamond set.

People in the auditorium checked their watches.

After several minutes The Daughters spread out to return to their metal folding chairs marked "NHS."

Honey White Bear-de la Rosa, looking like she might have poison ivy, holding the big book away from her fleshy chest with both hands, walked over to Nick.

He stepped up on the little stairs again, a quizzical look on his face for sure.

Honey shook her head.

"Nice try," she said, handing the book to Nick.

He took it and stepped down, paging through it to see what the schmuck had gone wrong.

Honey White Bear-de la Rosa, President Of The Daughters Of The Last Century, returned to the microphone and announced to the town, to the region, to the world, that for the first time in memory, The Daughters had rejected the new sophomore history textbook.

The town gasped.

The janitors leaning on brooms gasped. This would now take longer and they had shit to do.

The reporters in the first row hustled up, trying to talk to Honey, trying to interview Nick, as he plowed through them, up the middle aisle, as the high school band played loud, triumphant Neil Diamond music until he reached the back row and then stopped.

Nick barged outside to where Kamil slumped on the steps smoking.

Kamil asked him how did it go?

"The Easter Bunny! The god-damned fucking Easter Bunny. Oh, shit, shit, shit!" said Nick.

Nick accepted a cigarette.

He didn't feel like sitting though.

"I can't sit," he said.

Kamil continued to sit.

"So," said Kamil.

"Now what?"

"Now what what?" said Nick.

"They didn't take it."

"They didn't?" said Kamil.

"They usually do, right?"

"Yes, they usually do. They always do!" said Nick.

"I heard the music," said Kamil.

"Whoever controls the past controls the present, or the future, I forget," said Kamil.

"Or visa versa."

"Now the schmuck do I do!" said Nick, pulling hard on the smoke.

"Wanna go ridin' around? Get a quart a beer?" said Kamil.

"Nice day, we could go fishing. Worms at Dave's are marked down. It's been too hot, lots of them melted, but some are still good. Huh?"

"Nope, I gotta do somethin' about this," said Nick.

"Man, what do I do!"

He fired the butt at the grass, then tracked it down and stepped on it, ground it out to dust.

Nick looked up as the old wooden double doors shoved open and revealed a pissed Honey White Bear-de la Rosa.

She held her dress high and waltzed down the cement steps side-saddle.

"What the hell!" she said.

Nick felt her spit.

"I don't know. You could use last year's book," said Nick.

"No! We have a tradition!" said Honey White Bear-de la Rosa.

"And, it's not new."

"What?" said Kamil.

She turned on him like an attacker in the dairy aisle.

"The old history book!"

"Yep, it's old history," said Nick.

"This is the newest, the brand-newest hist'ry we've got, or that really exists, anywhere, right?" said Nick.

"Yep," said Kamil K.

"Why did you do that?" she pleaded, her hands in fists at her sides as turtle heads started to peak out the old wooden double doors to see if it was okay to go home now.

"Get back in there!"

Honey pointed with a long, pink fingernail and the heads shoved back in. The doors closed without sound.

"Let me see that again," she said.

Nick handed it over.

He motioned to Kamil to quick give him a cigarette, then passed it to Honey. She took it.

Honey sat on the steps, her dress all around her, turning each single page of the book, shaking her head, nodding at times, growling, moaning.

"Ohhh, God."

She finished and handed the book up to Nick.

"Are you sure about this, all these things?"

She looked back to Kamil.

He shrugged his shoulders.

"I'm not sure," she said.

"Some people don't like this, not very happy about it at all. You're a troublemaker. You're getting yourself in trouble and me in trouble and the whole bit."

Nick looked at Kamil.

Back at Honey.

"Then, you knew what was in here before today?" said Nick.

"Oh, yes, yes, yes, yes," she moaned, fired the butt at the sidewalk, and put her head in her hands.

"Are you sure?"

She looked up, her big hat askew, her dress taking up half of the goddamned cement school steps.

Nick looked up at Kamil, who shrugged again and looked away, up and down the street.

"Yep, 110 percent," said Nick.

"It's the gospel."

CHAPTER FORTY-TWO

"The American people deserve to know their own history."
— *James Fetzer*

Nick stood on his own front porch, his hands on his hips, staring as he often did toward the campus of the publishing house that he had managed for many years, either admiring it or gathering the courage to tackle another day.

He saw a big moving truck go past, down Hedge Road, toward the administration building, and then another.

"No!" he shouted as he stretched out his arms and leaped from the porch steps.

He landed in perfect position, a Russian folk dancer squat, and then shot up, out the gate and down the street, shouting and reaching.

"No! No! No!

"It's not ready! Not today!

"It's not time!"

The moving trucks, eighteen-wheeled semi's with the Bouton Fiflin Starcourt ... Mace Yovonovich-Fofonovich Banana-fana Momonovich emblem on the sides were lined up all around the semi-circle drive for most of the next week, hauling out of the buildings and pushing up inclines to place all of Nick Greene's publishing house into the trucks.

As the movers hauled out the vending machines in Martha and Mary's New Offices on ten dollies all in a row, Nick and Daisy, back from her honeymoon, sat on the cement bench and watched.

"Mr. Peabody's Coal Train," said Nick, not expecting Daisy to get it.

She sang the whole song softly twice to Nick as they sat watching giant trucks crawl past.

She found one of her old napkins under the bench, dabbed her own eyes and then handed it to Nick.

"Well, I guess it was theirs after all?" he said.

"Yep," said Daisy.

"Yep," said Mary and Martha at the same time.

Nick turned around and saw them, along with The Generals, Lori Groome, Deanno, Honey White Bear-de la Rosa, Janey, Katie, Harland Lombardi, Hess Bangor, Bobby Barkham, Blaze Thornpine, Max Karp, Eddie, the rest of the department managers and all the employees, stretching way back now as they walked up around the circle drive.

"So! We're screwed!" said Nick, loudly, as one of the big trucks moved past, changing gears, pulling slowly away.

"Pretty much," said Kamil, his elbow in the window, pulling up along the curb in the Pontiac.

"Maybe not," said Mary, edging closer with Martha at her elbow.

Mary sat on the edge of the bench, leaned forward, elbows on her knees to talk around Daisy, to Nick.

"Mr. Peabody didn't get all the coal, Neeky."

"Yep, pretty much," said Nick.

"Those trucks ... have you ever stood in the compartment of one of those trucks? When its empty? They hold a lot of stuff."

"A *lot* of stuff."

He tossed a rolled up ball of napkin at the sidewalk and watched it roll awkwardly away.

"It's over."

Martha moved over, in front of Mary, Daisy, to stand right in front of Nick and make him straighten up and look at her.

She wore her full which costume, a ball cap that said "Which", and a tight, white T-shirt with "Which" in bold black letters across her chest, from the days when she and Mary had to fight the whole town by themselves.

She stood with her feet shoulder-width apart, a good stance for a ballplayer, her hands on her hips.

"Follow me," said Martha.

She reached out.

Nick took her hand but did not budge.

"Please," she said.

He looked down again, wiggled his toes inside the black leather.

"These aren't really publishing boots are they?" he said to Daisy.

"No," she said.

"I thought it would make you feel better. You seemed to be having kind of a tough time."

Nick leaned over and kissed Daisy on the cheek.

"Okay, then," he said to Martha, still holding his hand.

"Let's go.

"Follow the yellow brick road!"

He stood and waved to everyone with his one free hand.

They all followed Martha and Mary and Nick in between them, walking along the campus sidewalk, over a bumpy lawn, to the ninth hole green, up, almost straight down, helping each other, through a sand trap, rough, to The Tower.

"I'm not sure I still have the key," said Nick.

"It's open," said Mary as she pulled on the old wooden door.

Martha and Mary led them inside, to the big first floor room, where there were two computers, one set of golf clubs and one vending machine, along with the flag to Hole Number Nine.

"The enchanted hole," said Nick.

"Yep," said Mary.

"Who put all this stuff in here?" said Nick, smiling, knowing the answer.

"The Easter Bunny!"

Martha and Mary put their arms in the air and shouted and Daisy and everyone else shouted as well.

"Samizzzdat," Mary and Martha hummed together, as they herded everyone out to sit on the nice, level area of the ninth green.

"You two!" Nick gave them a double high-five and turned to join the others headed on out.

They all sat on the green as Martha and Mary stood, walking amongst them, speaking, teaching.

They explained self-publishing and print on demand and desktop publishing as some complained that it was lunch time and what could they find for this many people to eat.

Martha smiled and sent a young boy to the one remaining vending machine.

He returned with his arms full and passed it out and all were filled.

"It's not really over until you quit," said Daisy to Nick, sitting right beside him on the green.

"I know, right?" he said.

CHAPTER FORTY-THREE

Samizdat:
Literally "self-publishing house"
Origin: Russian, literally, self-published from samo-self +
izdat, to publish. Izdatel'stvo: publishing house.

"Very, very nice."

Nick stood behind Lori Groome, watching her put the finishing touches on her new art on the window of the front door.

It said "Publishing House," in rainbow colors, and showing a birds-eye view of The Tower, and the winding river.

Nick went inside to his first floor office.

"Honey on line one!" said Daisy.

The floors of The Tower comprised all the departments, editing, research, writing, art, paper, font, margins & spacing. John Brown even had his own area for visiting focus groups. The gluers had been able to move into "the dungeon," a dark, damp basement area that seemed to be working perfectly for them.

The new sub-title bunker had been arranged in a closet on the second floor.

Martha and Mary worked the computers in their old top floor area with the skylight and wooden floors and their same old big desk and Folger's can.

* * *

Honey White Bear-de la Rosa organized the town.

She printed a regular schedule of New History Cakes to be delivered three times a day to The Publishing House, and women to do the laundry of the history book workers, and men to do repairs and fix-up on the publishing building.

Kamil K. sat in the semi-circle drive in the lime-green faded Pontiac with the motor running.

Randy the reporter and Langley Harmsworth took the airport shuttle to the airport for the flight to New York City. They traveled incognito and Randy talked the whole way, planning their Big Plan For The Big Surprise Expose Of Fulton Crampton And That Other Guy Who Was With Him.

Langley Harmsworth nodded her approval.

Her photographer nodded from his back.

Hess Bangor found a chair that he liked stashed in The Publishing House, and sat outside Nick's office, just next to Daisy's reception desk.

Blaze Thornpine formed a new social club, The Lone Gunmen, and took over the old Moose Lodge on Paradise Street that had been scheduled for destruction and a parking lot.

The old man wore a policeman's hat backwards as he sat in a tree by the front entrance as director of security operations.

His feet dangled, covered nicely by Nick's old publishing boots. He whittled a new spear or pool cue.

"Miss Principal Bordeaux," said Daisy, standing in Nick's doorway.

"Yep," said Nick, busy, looking down, figuring some things out.

"To see you.

"Don't blow it," said Daisy as she turned to smile at Miss Principal Bordeaux.

She pranced in, sat in the one metal folding chair, her hands folded primly in her lap.

Nick adjusted his Yankees cap like a cowpoke who has just seen the face of Jesus in a jelly doughnut.

"Well," he said.

"Yep," she said.

Nick noticed she was wearing one of Honey's new "We Support The Historians" yellow ribbons in her hair.

Miss Principal Bordeaux cleared her throat, swept some invisible thread from her dress, and explained how she had met with the school board in a special meeting just that morning.

And how they had decided they would in fact be requiring a whole new set of sophomore history textbooks ASAP, and would there still be time to place their order?

As Nick twirled around after walking Miss Principal Bordeaux to the door he winked at Daisy and began to hum "the coal train song."

Daisy winked back.

CHAPTER FORTY-FOUR

"History is the lie commonly agreed upon."

— *Voltaire*

D aisy waved to everyone from the passenger seat of Kamil's Pontiac. She tossed flowers and nine cousins fell upon them like hyenas on the walk.

Harland pressed hard to toot the horn and off they went in a cloud of smoke as everyone moseyed back inside the Utilitarian Church for The Big Sub-Title Banquet Post-History Cake For Dessert Ceremony.

Tomorrow would be The Big Pageant, with a float representing every chapter in The New Sophomore History 101 textbook.

It was supposed to rain and so Honey White Bear-de la Rosa had excused herself early from the banquet to go work in the theater and arrange all the floats on the turntable stage and then also the back hall waiting line.

Somehow she had to make it work.

She was just pulling on her leather work gloves when she saw The Generals, Eddie and Martha & Mary coming in the front door of the theater like a herd of elephants.

She smiled and turned to place a chrysanthemum on a tractor rim.

She gave them instructions and they began to fan out, pull wrenches from pockets, take off jackets, tie bandanas around heads, pull on gloves.

* * *

Usually the stout little delivery trucks with the brand new lettering and designs would wait until after The Big Pageant to leave the big parking lot in front of the main office, With The Whole Town Waving, Clapping And Cheering, but this was no ordinary year.

Nick balanced on the curb waving to each driver, saying thank you and good luck and go fast.

"You are doing important work!" he shouted to each.

"This book is very important!

"We are important!

"Yaaaayyyy!"

Truck after truck after truck left the parking lot, past Nick, into the street, headed for the highway and everywhere.

Perfect little trucks in a line down the road with little puffs of exhaust, put, put, put, just like in the children's story books.

Nick turned away after tasting the exhaust of the last one.

"Whatever," he said.

He took one step back toward the office and changed in mid-air to head on downtown, with a new limp.

He looked up at the sky and winked.

At least that was how the eagle imagined it all, as she swirled around and around, high up, and then closer and then high again.

One time, after a long time of swooping and swirling around the grass and the big trees and the nine hundred tree wood, and up by the pieces of wood and brick that might have at one time been something, at a piece of old pastry still in its paper wrapper, and metal and a white round something over by the curious diamond-shaped dirt, she came way back over here to rest by the river.

She pecked at something old, something pink, maybe an ear to a costume, and something shiny, that might have at one time been an eyelet for an ancient fishing pole.

ALLISON HEALY - ARTIST

Raised in the Northwoods of Minnesota, Allison developed a deep connection to the natural world as well as a great attention to detail, a theme that carries through much of her work. She left high school two years early and received an associate degree in liberal arts, with a focus in literature and fine art at the age of eighteen. Earning a Bachelor of Fine Arts degree in illustration from the Minneapolis College of Art & Design, she also spent some time abroad intensively studying illustration and graphic design at the University of Brighton, on the south coast of England. Her work has appeared on a range of publications, including but not limited to: book covers, children's books, magazines, album covers, greeting cards, and several applied graphics for various products. She is currently living and working in Boston, Massachusetts, where her studio is now based.

www.ingramcontent.com/pod-product-compliance
Lightning Source LLC
Chambersburg PA
CBHW030252130626
46549CB00002B/503